UNDER THE MAHOGANY TREE

A story of chess intrigue

Feng Ping

Published in Australia by

Heart Space Publications
PO Box 1190
Bakery Hill, Victoria, 3354, Australia
Tel +61 450260348
www.heartspacebooks.com
pat@heartspacebooks.com

Author Feng Ping

Whilst every care has been taken to check the accuracy of the
information in this book, the publisher cannot be held responsible for
any errors, omissions or originality.

Published in Melbourne, Australia in October 2021
ISBN: 978-0-6452761-0-7

ABOUT THE AUTHOR

Feng Ping was born in Shanxi province, China. She gained her Ph.D. at the University of Warsaw, where she studied International Relations with a focus on China's foreign policy towards Central Eastern European countries.

She plays chess, enjoys classical music, and reads widely.

This is her fourth book; *Four Legendary Women from Ancient China* (published by Heartspace Publications ISBN; 9780648921530). Her first published work was *Roads Seeking* and her second was *Love in Warsaw*. She wrote these in Poland during her studies.

楚河
炮
炮

PREFACE

The origin of Chinese chess can be traced back to the Zhou dynasty (1046 BC-256 BC). The game was initially popular among nobles and officers.

Modern Chess is believed to have originated in India. However, the way the Chinese play is different to that of Westerners (refer to appendix). Yet it is still very much a game of intrigue, where opponents strive for the initiative.

Chinese chess was not available to commoners until the Ming dynasty (1368 AD-1644 AD), in which period this story is set. It is a heroic, but tragic story about a chess master. The story has it that at the beginning of the Ming dynasty, the master of the Plum Valley Chess Club, Wang Siyi, played an important game with the founding emperor of the Ming dynasty, Zhu Yuanzhang. The aim of this match was to persuade the emperor to abolish his ban on commoners playing chess. Wang played knowing that he could lose his life, whether he won or lost.

Contents

CHAPTER ONE
THE GRAND MASTER, WANG SIYI

During the Yuan dynasty (1271 AD-1369 AD) in the southern part of China, a great chess master named Wang Siyi lived in the beautiful Plum Valley. This valley was once regarded as the most secluded place on earth. He ran a chess school to teach disciples the art of chess. As a recognised chess master, he had a long-held dream that ordinary people would also be able to play chess, and the game would no longer be restricted to the elite classes.

Outside the humble compound that served as Wang Siyi's chess school and home was a mahogany tree. It was gnarled and majestic, having stood for several hundred years.

It was under this tree where, weather permitting, Master Wang held class. For hours, he and his students sat under the canopy, while ants, beetles and bugs of all sorts traversed up and down the trunk, like traffic in and out of the capital on market day. Birds rested and fed, up high in the safety of the tall branches as they surveyed the distant landscape.

Often in times of reflection, Wang Siyi wondered how many old men like him had sheltered from the sun and pondered life under its hefty canopy. He loved the tree, and knew it had seen the travails and happiness of life. It was here that he determined that his peaceful life would not last long. At the end of the Yuan dynasty, warlords started another war, trying to divide the dynasty. In the beginning, Wang tried to ignore the warlords and their soldiers, striving to retain his life of dedication to chess.

Wang had many disciples. He was a generous man, giving instruction on chess, as well as how to be a good and wise human being. Chess and life were of similar form: one needed to think twice before leaping forward. One day, before the warlords divided the dynasty, one of his disciples asked him, "Master, how does one become a chess master who will be remembered throughout history?" Wang was lost for words momentarily, as he did not consider himself a chess master. He looked up into the tree as if inspiration sat on a low branch, ready to be plucked like a ripe apple.

He simply said, "Learning chess is a lifelong business. Only then, perhaps one becomes good enough to be considered a master."

In fact, it was not until he met his future son-in-law that Wang found his own answer to the question.

It happened that Wang saved the life of a young monk whose name was Dan Yu. To repay Master Wang for his kindness, Dan Yu decided to cease being a monk, and instead remained in the Valley to study Chinese chess under Wang.

Plum Valley was a place that derived its name from the plum-coloured wintersweet flowers that blanketed the mountainside and dales, blossoming in a variety of colours. Their fresh fragrance greeted the valley people and intoxicated them with their scent. It was a quiet place, free from worldly worries, a place to escape from the ongoing warfare.

Dan Yu spent most of his time leaning against the trunk of the mahogany tree, learning the game of chess and reading as many military strategy books as he could acquire. He was so dedicated that within a year, he was able to defeat all the other disciples. As custom dictated, he married the daughter of Wang Siyi.

However, the day came that while Master Wang was absent, a band of Mongols attacked Plum Valley. Most of the disciples were slaughtered, and only a few managed to escape.

On Wang's return to the valley he was confronted with devastation. Everything around the compound had been burnt. Only the mahogany tree stood imperious, over-looking the folly of man's lust for more. Dan Yu was numb with shock, and he trembled with anger.

He sunk to his knees and cried, "Oh, heaven! How can you treat our people this way? You are blind and too cruel to be God in Heaven!"

Wang was mortified, his face white as snow. He tried to comfort his son-in-law, "These are the ways of the world. Hardship, birth, old age, sickness. Death awaits us all. It is incontestable."

Da Yu looked at his father-in-law with anguish, "Father, why do we play chess when there are such problems in life. Does chess not trivialise life?"

This question had already haunted Wang. He felt a pang of conscience.

"Wisdom is gained by playing chess. It is a pleasant hobby in a time of peace. But not in troubled times. What do we fight for on the chessboard? The justice on the scales? Or for wisdom? Yes, that is a noble pursuit in peaceful times. But now, when the Mongols cruelly tread on us, what kind of chess game should we play? If we are still devoted to chess, as if nothing happened, what we do is no more than dragging out our feeble existence!... I can't do this anymore."

Wang Siyi was shocked and asked, "So, what are you to do?"

"I will join the army and fight on real battlefields to help purge the savages that squash us."

With these words, Dan Yu left Plum Valley and joined the rebellion to fight the Mongol invaders. He soon rose through the ranks and became a leader within the military. It was his chess skills and previous study of military strategy that had prepared him for leadership.

In 1368 AD, Zhu Yuanzhang gained control of the warlords and expelled the Mongol invaders. He was the first emperor of the Ming Dynasty China.

By this time, Dan Yu had returned from the battlefields. While as a commander he confiscated all the treasures he had gained in battle, this was not to line his own pockets, but to be retained in a secret place in case the Mongols returned. The treasure would be used to fund armies. He passed on the treasure to his master, Wang Si, who he knew he could trust. Wang Si hid the treasures in a mountain cave in the valley. Dan Yu left to help rebuild the country and disappears from our story.

One of Emperor Zhu Yuanzhang's first tasks was to set up a set of rules and regulations to promote the recovery of the country. As part of this, he authorised a complete ban on the playing of chess. He felt that chess prevented the people from giving him the adulation he deserved. Yet he did not want to be seen as the reason for the banning of the game. He therefore concocted a plan, issuing an imperial edict that he would hold a chess competition. For the competition, he ordered that each chess piece was to be made of a large, heavy piece of stone. A large area of ground was marked out as the chess board. To play, each player had to drag the pieces over the rough ground. Soon, exhaustion set in. It was only a matter of hours before blood dripped on the stone pieces from wounds attained. The players became agitated and aggressive with each other.

Seeing this unbecoming scene, Emperor Zhu issued a second imperial edict banning the playing of chess because chess made people combative. The penalty for those who were caught playing was death.

Wang, in Plum Valley, worried all chess players would be in danger. Preparing for the worst, the first thing he did was to dismiss his disciples, except his favourite, Chong Xu. He said to his other disciples, "It's too dangerous for you to remain here to continue your lessons. You must leave and return home."

The young men were reluctant to leave. They wept and begged their master to allow them to stay, but seeing that he had made his mind up they had no choice but to pack their belongings, leaving the serenity of Plum Valley for the chaotic world beyond.

Before they departed, the disciples often discussed the rumors of there being treasure, though they dare not ask their master about it. Before the disciples went their separate ways, one of them overheard a private conversation between Wang Si and Chong Xu about the creation of a manual which would contain a code leading to the treasure. One of the disciples, Rou Zengnan, constantly conjectured about the treasure and longed to get his hands on the manual, but it had not been completed by then.

Wang's next project was to finish documenting his lifelong chess-learning experience in a manual called *The Secret under the Mahogany Tree.* He had long intended to write a chess manual and was now able to complete it with the help of his most faithful and talented disciple, Chong Xu. This they did together, sitting for weeks under the mahogany tree, brush ready as they enacted games and strategy. When they first started writing the manual, the tree above them was covered in abundant foliage, but by the time they had finished, it was rust coloured with falling leaves. It seemed as if the end of its season reflected the end of Wang Siyi's season.

Special attention was paid to the embedding of a code as to where the treasure was hidden in the manual. The code must appear to be meaningless to anyone other than a chess master of integrity.

Several years after the chess ban, Wang knew the time had come for him to appeal to the Emperor. It was then that he instructed Chong Xu to look after the secret manual. Addressing him gravely and earnestly Wang reiterated, "This manual documents my life of chess; every learnt move, as well as the where-abouts of the treasure. I'm to leave the Valley to petition the Emperor. I am not likely to return. When the time comes, pass the book on to a worthy chess player, one gifted and possessing integrity."

"Master!" Chong Xu said as he held back tears. He knew the implications of this trip and that his master was likely to face death. It was likely this would be the last time he would see his master.

After saying an emotional farewell to his family and friends, Master Wang started the journey to the Ming dynasty's capital.

After a while, Wang was finally permitted to meet with the Emperor. The emperor sat on the golden throne, holding a white feathered fan, looking majestic. Snake-like eyes watched from a protruding forehead, and he licked his big rubbery lips every few seconds. He looked down at Wang Siyi, who was kneeling in front of him, and nonchalantly asked, "Wang Siyi, what do you have to say for yourself?"

Wang nodded his head, his eyes downcast but with his back determinedly straight, "My Lord, people should be allowed the joy of chess, both commoners and the upper-class alike!"

"You are brave to come here and challenge my orders!"

Wang Siyi continued. He would not back down now, "I do not mean to challenge, but to express my humble opinion."

"Chess is not good for the dynasty. People derive grandiose ideas from thinking they can take lessons from the board and gain an upper-hand in matters of importance. Oh no, we won't allow that to happen."

"My Lord, even if people do not play on the chessboard, aren't people playing with strategic moves all the time?" Wang Siyi said, his countenance unchanged.

Zhu Yuanzhaung was confused and wondered if there was a touch of sedition in the words, asking, "What are you suggesting?"

"Playing chess is no different to making everyday decisions. My Lord, you are just like the king on the chessboard, and the pieces your citizens, who play their role to do your bidding. If the entire dynasty is to work well, each person has to perform his or her duties honestly. Then, as the king, you have the support of all your people."

"No, this is not how it is. War has only left our door and peace has just been restored. What people need to do is to toil in the fields and rebuild the country. This is the only way to keep the dynasty rich and prosperous. If everyone gives up their job to devote themselves to the game of chess, hunger will follow."

"My Lord, forgive me for saying so, but chess is a great treasure bequeathed to us by our ancestors. And, yes, it does help people in their daily lives. We need to allow its spirit to carry forward for the benefit of our descendants." Wang hesitated briefly but emboldened, continued, "Banning the playing of chess is a travesty to our people and ancestors."

There was silence while the emperor considered these words, until Wang boldly asked, "I suggest you and I play a game of chess, Your Majesty."

Momentarily, Emperor Zhu was touched by Wang Siyi's staunch uprightness. Was he wrong to ban chess? Now he was torn as to whether to follow his path or to listen to Wang. Thinking of himself as a fair and enlightened leader, he finally responded, "Okay, we shall play, with small pieces." Zhu Yuanzhang laughed drily, thinking of the other chess players that became exhausted when they played with the large stone pieces. By allowing the small pieces, Zhu Yuanzhang was sparing Wang Siyi's life.

However, Wang Siyi knew that the mood of the emperor was changeable. If Zhu Yuanzhang laughed all the world had to humour him, but if he was angry there would be a river of blood flowing across the dynasty. Wang had already determined to sacrifice his life for the sake of gaining a promise from the emperor, and said with determination, "I will play with heavy stone pieces, and play for both parties. Instruct your eunuch to pass on to me your moves, I will drag the heavy pieces. For me, I propose death if I lose. But if I win, I beg you, Sir, to swear that you will revoke the ban on chess."

Zhu Yuanzhang chuckled and agreed with Wang Siyi's proposal. The game started with Wang Siyi the only person on the board, amid very large pieces. Zhu Yuanzhang sat in regal splendour in chair that had been placed under a Dawn Redwood that offered deep shade.

"Cannon b2rd moves to the cannon g6thc," came the eunuch's voice. Wang Siyi moved the heavy piece according to the eunuch's instructions. Wang Siyi could have ended the game quickly, but delayed its end for a couple of reasons. For one, if he won too easily, the emperor would lose face, and who knew what that could result in. The other reason — the main reason — was that Wang Siyi knew he would only be successful in his quest to have the ban lifted if he perished. Being humble, he did not wish to be become a martyr, but he would do what was necessary. The game continued, move after move, and Wang Siyi eventually became exhausted. Several times, he clutched at his heart. He sweated profusely, but continued without drinking even a sip of water.

Wang won the game. However, he experienced a massive wave of pain in his chest and collapsed on a stone piece and died. Zhu Yuanzhang bent over the corpse, and clapped his hands to summon his aide, "Make sure he is given an elaborate funeral and a good headstone. From now on he shall be regarded as the most famous Chess Master of our time."

ප ప ප ප ප ප

Zhu Yuanzhang lifted the ban on chess. From then on, playing chess became popular among the common people. Many chess clubs opened all over the kingdom.

In the early period of the Ming dynasty, life was peaceful. However, for many years, no other chess master emerged.

CHAPTER TWO
LEAVING THE PLUM VALLEY FOR THE SAKE OF A BEAUTIFUL WOMAN

Along the Qinhuai River in the capital, business thrived. The streets were always crowded. Red paper lanterns, lit at night, reflected on the river, small ripples twinkled in the background. The singing of entertainment girls could be heard. Dragon boats rowed through the deep water, causing small waves on the sluggish river's surface. A light breeze caressed thin willows, which in turn swayed like beautiful women dancing on tiptoe. The intoxicating fragrance of flowers greeted all. Such richness and extravagance could be compared with the famous picture, *Along the River During the Qingming Festival* by Zhang Zeduan, painted in the Song dynasty (960 AD–1279 AD). Perhaps it was even richer than that.

Since Emperor Zhu Yuanzhang had lifted the chess ban, chess clubs had sprung up like bamboo shoots after rain. Some were small, others large, but all were competitive with each other. Most of the players were dedicated. Two clubs stood out among thousands of competitors. One was the *Plum Valley Chess Club*, and the other was *Happiness Chess Club*. Their masters were masters of note, Jin Tieling and Wang Wengfeng.

When young, both Jin Tieling and Wang Wengfeng had been disciples of Chong Xu, the favourite disciple of Grand Master Wang Siyi. It was he who still retained the chess manual *The Secret under the Mahogany tree*. The three would sit under the mahogany tree, Chong Xu taking up Master Wang's former position, leaning against the wide trunk of the tree.

Back in the Plum Valley times, Jin and Wang were friends, sworn brothers. They had spent three carefree years studying chess, which proved to be the happiest and the most secluded time for both men.

After Wang Siyi died in the chess duel with the emperor, Chong Xu removed himself from the vanities of life and the hypocrisy of the world. He became a Taoist monk. Throughout his life, Chong Xu only accepted two disciples, Jin Tieling and Wang Wengfeng, because both were intelligent and diligent. Neither talked too much, and both attentively listened to their master. Chong Xu often related to them the story of Wang Siyi and his determination to have chess open to all, even though it led to his death. When he did, the memory of his master flooded back to him, and he would say in a dream-like way, "He taught me, 'If you want to play chess and become a master, you must have determination and integrity.'"

Wang Wengfeng's chess style was steadfast and stable, while Jin Tieling's was quite the opposite, free and expansive. Jin Tieling moved the pieces quite fast, almost instinctively. When Wang Wengfeng moved, he would contemplate for some time to ensure his strategy was without risk. He was never willing to abandon a piece for the sake of gaining an advantage.

For both students, the three years seemed to pass in the blink of an eye. It was not an easy time, living like hermits, and spending hours under the tree. Chong Xu had them read many military texts, such as *The Art of War*, and the *I Ching*. Both dreamt of becoming a Grand Master like Wang Siyi.

Chong Xu would always remind his disciples that to learn to play chess well, they needed to learn how to become good humans first. Learning chess was not much different from learning Kung Fu, where a chivalrous spirit was required. They needed to have a high moral standard, and be able to judge right from wrong.

The famous but secluded Plum Valley was located not far from the capital. With spring coming, the mountaintop snow began to thaw. The melted snow trickled into small streams. This was the most beautiful season, late February, where sweet fragrances could be smelled almost everywhere and the hills and valleys were decorated with colour. The plum flower that grew at this time was one of the three plants that weathered winter well and was greatly favoured by Chinese scholars. This is because of the hardiness of the wintersweet flower – they survived the cold of the early spring, trying their best to blossom. Just as an ancient Chinese poet once said, *The sweet winter flowers are unwilling to blossom first in the spring, but they do. Being the queen of flowers, the plum wintersweet flower is greatly admired and envied by hundreds of other flowers.*

Jin Tieling and Wang Wengfeng often walked with their master in this beautiful scenery and devoted great attention to nature, attempting to discover the secrets of the universe, all to enhance their chess skills. Scanning the high mountains and listening to bubbling brooks, they were totally engrossed in nature.

Both desired to see the secret manual *The Secret under the Mahogany tree*. Occasionally, when they hinted to their master, either in passing or joking, Chong Xu would smile mysteriously, saying "It's not time yet."

The disciples were miffed every time they heard this. They dreamt of fame being bestowed upon them as real chess masters, and were keen to see the manual to help them achieve this goal.

One day, when Chong Xu was away from the valley for a few days, Wang Wengfeng and Jin Tieling found themselves with some time on their hands. The two played chess for a while, however, the more they played, the more restless and impatient they grew. They were usually well-matched. Jin Tieling won this game and scoffed, "Ha-ha, why did you lose your horse so easily in the beginning? You seemed absent-minded today."

Wang Wengfeng replied, "Brother, you have made great strides in your chess skills. I couldn't motivate myself and kept thinking that in a few years' time I won't be able to match your skill."

Tieling tried to mollify his friend and said, "Nonsense, it's just because you are feeling low. We are equal in skill."

Wengfeng sighed, "To be truthful, I'm tired of this dull valley. I would love a day out in the city. What about you?"

Jin Tieling was stunned but realised he liked the idea. "Yes, I do!"

Wengfeng smiled, "Let's go. Life is too short to not have fun."

The two friends shook hands in agreement and set off on their journey out of the valley. They went directly to the capital of the Ming dynasty, and were amazed at its prosperity and grandeur, especially after the austerity of the valley. People of all classes filled the streets. Many chess clubs and tea houses were full to the brim.

Seeing a sign *The Talented Chess Club* inscribed on a plaque, the boys decided to enter the club. They played some games with a few of the guests and won some money. The master of the club was Rou Zengnan, who was now elderly, but not so old that he did not notice the two young men. He surreptitiously appraised their skill whilst they played, and noticed they had a certain air about them. Wandering over to them he asked with a smile, "Boys, who is your master?"

Wengfeng smiled, "We are nobodies, never mind our master." After collecting their money, they left the club, carelessly humming a happy tune.

Rou Zengnan, you may remember was one of the disciples driven out of the Plum Valley by Wang Siyi when the emperor banned chess. Judging by these two young men's skills, Rou Zengnan was able to determine that they were descendants of the Wang Siyi School. He was alarmed and again thought of the treasure code in the manual. He decided to keep an eye out for these two young men and hope to find an opportunity to find the location of the manual.

Tieling and Wengfeng tried their luck in other chess clubs and ended up winning more games. Wengfeng said to Tieling half-jokingly, "That was easy enough."

"It's great fun," sighed his friend, "but we won our games too easily. It's just like hunting tortoises."

"Let's have a drink." Wengfeng suggested whilst playing with some coins in his hand.

After finding an establishment, and with a drink in hand, Wengfeng said, "I have an idea. Let's remain in the capital and open our own chess clubs? Would it not be wise to start a business in this busy capital?"

Tieling opened his mouth, quite speechless. He stammered after a moments pause, "That's a big thing. Let me think it over."

"Okay. Come drink up. Let's go and meet some ladies."

"Ladies?" Tieling repeated as if the word conjured up alien creatures, "What for?"

"You don't want to be a monk, do you?"

"No, of course not."

"Then follow me!" Wengfeng laughed. A mischievous light flashed in his eyes.

Before he went to Plum Valley to study chess, Wang Wengfeng was a talented scholar from a middle-class family. Young as he was, before he studied chess with Chong Xu, he had visited many famous entertainment houses in the capital, enjoying their pleasures while flinging money around. His family members despaired about his extravagance. But then Wengfeng met an old man who happened to be good at chess, and he became so engrossed with the game that he miraculously changed his ways. He told his father that he wanted to learn the masterful game. His father was both happy and surprised that his prodigal son had changed his behaviour. His father sent Wengfeng to the purest place in the region, the Plum Valley, to learn chess from master Chong Xu, the only remaining disciple of Wang Siyi.

As for Tieling, it was a different story. He was born to a common family, to parents who battled to support the family. Tieling's father played chess and encouraged his son to learn. Realising that he was interested, he sent Tieling to Plum Valley to improve his chess skills.

Tieling followed Wengfeng blindly down a street where men swarmed outside a well-presented building. Above the building's gate, the plaque announced in bold golden Chinese characters, *Pleasurable Entertainment, the Place of Beauties.*

This happened to be one of the most famous brothels in the capital. They boasted that they employed the most beautiful girl, whose name was Wen Wen. She was renowned not only for her beauty, but also for her dancing and music-making. When she danced, it seemed as if a butterfly had taken form. Her waist was slender, like a sapling. For now, Wen Wen was able to make her living as a musician and dancer, rather than selling her body. She was born into a scholarly family and had education. However, the prospects of the family plundered, and Wen Wen was sold to the brothel by her alcoholic brother. Her beauty was so distinct, and her movement so exquisite, that she became the drawcard of the brothel. The procuress carefully protected her from being used or manhandled, as while the girl remained pure, she would be a money-spinner. Many well-to-do men paid Wen Wen a visit just to catch a glance of the famous beauty and watch her exotic dancing, singing, and the playing of her Guqin (a Chinese string instrument).

However, flowers wither too easily, and women lose the blossom of youth too fast. Beauty can never escape the killing hand of time. Wen Wen knew she survive because of her beauty and was sober enough to know she would be cast away like a wilted flower as soon as her first wrinkle appeared. She agonised about her future. Quite alone, in her tiny room, Wen Wen played her Guqin whenever sadness overwhelmed her. She played one tune again and again until a string broke. She could not continue, however, the light of hope in her mind had rekindled. She still nurtured a hope that one day, the wheel of fortune would change, and she would leave this dirty place. All she wanted was a simple life, to be a good man's wife, and to raise children. But she would have to pay out her madam out first!

Feeling listless, Wen Wen wandered downstairs to make herself a cup of tea, when she came face to face with two handsome young men. Instantly, she could see they were not the same as regular patrons, vulgar and with the stink of money.

Wengfeng and Tieling were stunned. Residing in Plum Valley for almost three years, they had never seen such a girl, with her radiance and beauty. *What possessed these two clean young men to come into this smoky den of corruption? They looked as pure as the driven snow, goggle-eyed with their jaws hanging open, speechless.* Living in that establishment had sharpened her wits, and she was first to recover, and so with laughing eyes, she mocked, "Country bumpkins? It's bad manners to stare." Wen Wen laughed, using a fan to half-cover her face.

"We've just dropped in… to look… um… um." Wengfeng stammered for both of them, his heart pounding hard. Tieling could not even stammer.

Seeing those two young men, so different from the other men she normally entertained, she invited them into a small parlour, telling them they had to buy a drink if they were to stay in this establishment. The two obediently followed her, heads lowered and pulses racing. In the parlour, both stood dumbly against the wall as if they were about to be shot by a firing squad. Amused, Wen Wen burst out laughing, "Who are you two? What do you do for living?"

Finding some composure, Wengfeng said, "We are chess disciples from Plum Valley. Have you heard of Plum Valley, Miss?"

"The Plum Valley?" Wen Wen's eyes lit up on hearing the news. "Are you disciples of the Wang Siyi School of chess?"

"We are. He was our Grand Master."

"Disciples of the Wang Siyi tradition!" Wen Wen bowed with profound respect. However, when she raised her head, tears were streaming down her face. The two boys were astounded. They could not understand where her sudden sadness came from.

"What saddens you, Miss?" asked Tieling with concern, finally finding his voice.

Wen Wen sat at her Guqin and started strumming the instrument as she spoke. She began to narrate her story, "When I was young, I did not know of sorrow. I was born into wealth. With the rise and fall of fortune, my family's wealth declined. My brother, now the head of the family, sold me to this place." On saying this, Wen Wen blushed as she had lost face.

"Destiny is not your fault, especially for a woman of breeding like you." Tieling said with righteous and youthful indignation. He blurted out, "You have been mistreated by your brother." Wen Wen smiled wanly and said nothing. She was grateful for Tieling's kindness.

Emboldened, he continued, "Most well-to-do-women spend their time in their room, never leaving. They just waste their time and youth."

"But I am also wasting my youth, only in a different way." Wen Wen said, blushing again. Both Tieling and Wengfeng looked at each other and said nothing more. Wen Wen continued playing two more pieces of music for them. Both men felt their heart going out to this young woman, and a deep sense of pity overwhelmed them. They had fallen in love with her.

Later, they agreed that they would each open a chess club and earn enough money to release Wen Wen from that dirty place. Then, they would ask her to marry one of them. They wanted to find their place in this colossal world, and secure the happiness of this beautiful young woman. If they could not save Wen Wen from her troubled situation, they would lose face and would never play chess again.

The men hurried back to Plum Valley. It was early evening, and the sun was low on the horizon, blazing like a flame underneath the clouds. It was so quiet and secluded that they could hear their footsteps echoing as they walked. The brook bubbled along, happily as usual. Late bird songs soothed. When they arrived, they saw their master, Chong Xu, sweeping the steps. Chong Xu interrupted his work and waited for his two disciples. He could see a change in them. *All was the same in the valley, but the two returning men were different. This beautiful and quiet landscapes would no longer satisfy them after the noisy and vibrant city.*

Their master made green tea for his disciples and himself. Facing their master, they were exhilarated but nervous. Chong Xu started the conversation first, "A few days ago I went out of the valley for business, and so you sneak out behind my back. Does the world outside appeal so much to you?" The two men nodded their heads, feeling ashamed. They did not want to lie. They briefly told him of their plan to help others learn chess. They did not mention Wen Wen.

Perceiving this before they spoke, Chong Xu said, "It seems that your time in this valley is over. You are both men and can make your own decisions. Though you will cease training before mastery, at least you do play well. Continue with your practice. Keep the philosophy of chess and life in mind… even if your tune is sad, it does not mean that you are overwhelmed with sorrow. Even if your chess games are good, it does not mean you are wise. We learn to play chess not to compete with others who seem better than us, but to fight for what is right. Sometimes, it's better to allow nature to take its course. And sometimes destiny calls."

Tieling and Wengfeng looked at each other and said nothing. Both felt ashamed — they knew they had let their master down. Master Chong Xu continued, "I release you. You are free to leave. It is good of you to promote the art of chess among the common people." The young men's eyes brimmed with tears.

That night, the two young men found sleep hard to come by, as the next day they would leave the valley. They feared the unknown. The world, with its myriad temptations, excited and horrified them at the same time.

While Tieling was packaging his few things, there was a knock on the door.

"Master!"

Chong Xu gestured for him to be quiet, "As my parting gift to you, I pass on Grand Master Wang Siyi's treatise, *The Secret under the Mahogany tree*, to you."

Tieling took the heavy volume with reverence. The weight was more than the pages. He moved a shaking hand over the words on the cover, *The Secret under the Mahogany tree*. Never did he consider himself worthy of this priceless gift. He trembled with gratitude and humility.

"Master, why me. Why not Wengfeng?"

"You are the correct choice. Only an exceptionally upright man can be the custodian of this manual. You must look after Wang Si's life work with all your heart. You are free to decide whether to pass this manual to another worthy person. But be careful, never let the manual fall into the hands of the evil minded or greedy."

"Thank you, Master." Suddenly, Tieling blushed, "Master, I must confess... there is a girl."

To Tieling's surprise Chong Xu chuckled, saying "Well if you had made her promises, and she is worthy, you need to keep your word. A gentleman never breaks a woman's heart. If you disregard her birth and past, and accept her wholeheartedly, it can only prove that you are a man of a conscience. Integrity is the basis of chess and life. I am proud of you. I trust your judgment. You are wise and good enough to pick out the pearl from the sand."

"Master..." Tieling was deeply touched and hesitated for a moment, "I am afraid that Wengfeng is also in love with the same girl."

Chong Xu was amused, remembering his younger days. His smiled reassured, "Nature has its own way."

In this way, Tieling and Wengfeng left the Valley to enter the world of ordinary people. As they parted from their master, full of emotion, Chong Xu told them that he would also be leaving the valley. He would live the life of a reclusive monk in some quiet corner of the world. Neither they nor anyone else would ever be able to find him. So, this was to be their final farewell.

The two friends headed back towards the capital city. Both were silent, content to let their mind's anxiously ponder what would become of them in the future, until Wengfeng sighed and said to Tieling, "It's a pity we left the Valley without Master allowing us to look at the manual of *The Secret under the Mahogany tree.*"

Tieling hesitated before saying, "Brother, last night when I was packing, Master came to me. He gave the manual to me to look after."

"What! I must look at it."

They sat under a tree, where Tieling took the book out and gently opened its cover. Sitting side by side, they turned each page, totally absorbed. The book had two parts, *gaining the initiative* was the main theme of the first volume, and *losing the initiative* the leitmotif of the second.

Whilst browsing the manual, a sense of jealousy swept over Wengfeng, *why did Master choose Tieling? Did Master not know that he had more potential than Tieling, though at the moment Tieling was equal with him? And as he had more financial support to open a chess club than Tieling, Master should therefore have placed the manual in his hands.*

As they closed the book, Tieling saw the disappointment in his friend's face. Feeling guilty, and in a moment of weakness he suggested, "Why don't we share the book? I'll keep the first volume *Gaining the initiative,* and you the second *Loosing the initiative?*"

Wengfeng thought, *Now Tieling is acting as if he is concerned for me, showing superiority of his character. But I will accept this offer.* With these thoughts Wengfeng hid his anger under a broad smile and said, "Thank you."

"It's my pleasure. Friendship must multiply joy and divide grief." Tieling laughed loudly and sincerely.

They continued walking and lapsed back into silence. Tieling was anxious to return and help Wen Wen as soon as possible. His intention was to be loyal and act with integrity, whether she chose him or not.

When they were about to separate company, not wanting to be obligated for receiving half the manual, Wengfeng gave Tieling some money to put towards opening a small chess club. The two friends embraced before going their different ways, uncertain of their future.

CHAPTER THREE
MARRIAGE

Tieling lost no time in getting his club going. It was a small club, with only a few tables and chess sets placed on the street. Nevertheless, it was a start. For nostalgia's sake, he named it *The Plum Valley Chess Club*, and used the image of the big mahogany tree as the logo. He missed the valley and the old man Chong Xu.

Wengfeng had a different philosophy. He did not miss the past as he was too self-absorbed. With family money behind him, he opened what was to be the biggest club in the city. He named it *The Happiness Chess Club* because of his desire for a hedonistic lifestyle. He quickly resumed his previous carefree life.

Both Tieling and Wengfeng attracted chess students and playing guests. Each visited Wen Wen in the brothel. At first Wen Wen was bemused as she never expected to meet the two again. Their visits gave her hope for a better future. She suffered great emotional anguish because of her virtual slavery. To entertain the guests, she would wear a false smile while writing poems for individual men. But the moment they left, with savage pleasure, she threw the poems into the fire and watch the flames devour them, as if it would burn everything that was dirty to ashes. She despised the men who wanted to paw her. But until the two boys arrived, there were none who would pity her for her misfortunes.

On Wengfeng's third visit to Wen Wen, after they had settled down, Wen Wen noticed herself in the copper mirror. She sighed with self-pity. Concerned, Wengfeng asked, "Why such a sad look and a sigh?" As he went over to her, Wen Wen looked up. He looked so handsome and confident. Wengfeng held her tight in his arms, trying to comfort her.

The next morning, still in bed, Wen Wen took out a handkerchief that she embroidered after first meeting Wang Wengfeng. She had fallen in love with him at first sight. She had embroidered a pair of lovebirds, even though she did not expect to meet him again. She gave the handkerchief to Wengfeng after this night of happiness. Wengfeng kissed the handkerchief warmly and smiled at her.

Wen Wen, with seriousness and knitted brows asked, "When are we to be married?"

"Of course," Wengfeng said sheepishly, "I need to talk to my father first." He felt a little empty when he thought of his father.

"Then, I take it we are engaged. You… you will keep your promise?" Wen Wen gazed into Wengfeng's eyes, trying to penetrate his heart, searching for the truth.

"It will be alright." Wengfeng hugged Wen Wen tight to his chest. Then carefully put the handkerchief into his pocket.

When Wengfeng returned home, he asked his father for a word. When he told him about marrying Wen Wen, his father exploded, "A seed of sin! How dare you want to bring a failed woman into our home? You must either be a fool or mad. And why have you come back from Plum Valley? Didn't you learn anything from your master? You can never make a crab walk straight."

Wengfeng was intimidated by his father's outburst. "Sorry, father. You are correct. As for chess, I am devoting time to continue improving my skills. Because of my ability I was even given half of the volume of *The Secret under the Mahogany tree*. This was given to me by my master." Wengfeng said sheepishly.

"Good... good. Now, about your marriage. To a man with such position and prospects as yours, how can you degrade yourself by marrying a failed woman? Your marriage has already been arranged. You are going to marry Miss Zhang." His father said this with indisputable authority.

"Do you mean the daughter of Senior official Zhang?" There flashed a wolfish light in Wengfeng's eyes. His heart was beating hard again.

"Yes, exactly." The father looked at his son with curiosity, "Well...?"

Wengfeng was about to grumble but restrained himself, embarrassed. He sank into deep thought, and calculated quickly whether his love for Wen Wen mattered enough for him to sacrifice such a good match as Miss Zhang. The answer was obviously 'No'. As to Wen Wen, well... she would manage.

Old Wang knew his son well, perceiving that his son had agreed to the marriage but was reluctant to acknowledge it, afraid of losing face. Old Wang smoothed his moustache and said, "Let's think about how to grow your chess club." Wengfeng nodded his head and retreated.

The moment Wengfeng left his father's room, he was sentimental. From love last night, to today' harshness, he had come to understand more about life. Sometimes people are unable to make the choices they want because love was just romance. Reality was cruel. People had to compromise. He had to be realistic.

He asked Tieling to have a drink with him in a wine bar. Sitting and drinking in the noisy bar, the two friends were talking and laughing just like before. "How's your chess club going?" Wengfeng asked.

"So so. With the little money I had and what you gave me I had to start small. Several students have applied, and it's growing. Thank you for the money."

Then Wengfeng asked, "Have you met with Wen Wen recently?"

"Yes, once. But I won't visit often." Tieling said blushing.

"Are you kidding me? Why?"

Tieling suddenly turned serious, and his generous smile disappeared, "Well, indeed, you are the only person in her heart. She seemed to be waiting for you."

Under Tieling's piercing gaze, Wengfeng felt his cheeks burn with shame. He choked and stammered, "There is no future for us. I have to marry someone else."

"What?" Tieling banged his hands on the bar, and exclaimed in anger, his voice carrying far above the noise of the room, "You monster! You could just as soon stab her with a dagger!" Wengfeng felt pangs of guilt, but reason governed his sensibilities. He forced a smile, and said resolutely but harshly, "Sometimes, people are not born to be together. Forgive me Tieling. I know you now look down upon me and regard me as swine. But you do not know my position."

Tieling narrowed his eyes and looked at Wengfeng, who seemed dispirited. He shrugged his shoulders and said, "I feel sorry for her."

There flashed a light in Wengfeng's eyes. Seeing Tieling's anger disappearing, he asked, "Will you do me a favour?"

"What?" Tieling asked with suspicion.

"Explain this to Wen Wen for me."

"Alas. How can that be done? You will have broken her heart, and you want me to fix it. I will. Not for you, but I will do it for her."

Wengfeng took out the handkerchief from his bag and passed it to Tieling, saying, "Please give this back to her… Tell her I am sorry…"

Tieling felt its softness and smelt her perfume lingering on it. *What a thing to cherish. Why would Wen Wen prefer Wang Wengfeng to him?*

Jin Tieling immediately went to the whorehouse, reluctantly, with the silk handkerchief in his hands. He kept wondering how he was to explain this to Wen Wen.

Wen Wen opened the door when she saw Tieling arrive. She hoped that he brought good news from Wang Wengfeng. She greeted him with a hopeful smile, until she noticed his gloomy face. His expression spoke more than words. Her heart turned cold knowing her fate. That as she aged, the madam would sell her body, which was the same as selling her soul. Tears cascaded down her face.

Tieling took her hands in his, wishing to console her. He could not bear seeing Wen Wen with her tear-filled eyes. He passed her the handkerchief. Receiving it Wen Wen felt an impulse to tear it into pieces, but Tieling stopped her. He wiped the tears off her face with his fingers. In a tender voice, and giddy with emotion he asked, "Will you marry me? I love you." Wen Wen, taken aback, wiped her eyes with the handkerchief to scrutinised his face. She could tell that he was serious. Emotion coursed through her, a mix of happiness, sadness, disappointment, relief, and surprise. She could not speak.

He continued, "If you are willing to marry me, I promise to give you security and all that you need, though I am not rich." Still, she studied his face. He did not look like a man who would cheat women with delusive promises. He would be as good as his word. She nodded her head, *yes*. In great confusion she did not know if she should be happy or sad.

The next day he took out all the savings that he had made since opening the chess club, along with some money he borrowed from friends, and returned to meet the procuress. She could see this young man was desperate for this girl, and so drove a hard bargain. She pushed for a higher price, but when she was sure she has consumed all the funds he had, she agreed.

Tieling and Wen Wen had a small but happy wedding, which created interest among the inhabitants of the capital. The beauty had finally found a home. People believed that Tieling and Wen Wen were a good match.

Of course, Wengfeng heard about the wedding and felt a flame of envy. He was jealous, not only because Jin Tieling married Wen Wen, whom he loved, but also because Tieling had done what he lacked the courage to do. Tieling was a mirror, reflecting all his character weakness. In a moment of rare honesty, he understood why Chong Xu gave the manual to Jin Tieling, and not to him. It was because the master had already seen something worthy in Tieling's character that he himself lacked.

At the very moment Tieling lifted the red bridal veil from Wen Wen's face, Wengfeng furiously smashed the wine cup from which he was drinking. During that first night of marriage between Tieling and Wen Wen, Wengfeng got drunk and walked to and fro in his room, unable to sleep.

The next morning, Wengfeng was still bad-tempered and swore at his servant. From that day on, Wengfeng considered Jin Tieling his enemy. He would seek revenge. He would wait for the perfect opportunity.

$\approx$ $\approx$ $\approx$ $\approx$ $\approx$ $\approx$

Slowly but surely, *The Plum Valley Chess Club* expanded, fuelled by Tieling's continuous diligent effort. He taught his disciples with respect and dignity, both on the chess board and off. He taught his students that it was necessary for each chess player to nurture his chivalrous spirit and to develop a scholarly groundwork so that one was farsighted enough to foresee many steps ahead in the game, as well as in life.

Wengfeng's *Happiness Chess Club* increased his fortune as he only allowed wealthy members, compared with the *Plum Valley Chess Club*, whose visitors were mostly common people. Wengfeng's club was frequently visited by eminent scholars and high-ranked officials. They came to have fun, play chess, and discuss politics. Wengfeng, ever the entrepreneur, had installed an entertainment service, which included a tea house, a small theatre, and a relaxation room.

The two friends, once sworn brothers, now enemies, and their two respective chess clubs, became fierce rivals.

CHAPTER FOUR
JIN XIAOMEI

Jin Xiaomei was the daughter of Wen and Tieling. By now Tieling and Wen Wen were a middle-aged couple, and Jin Xiaomei was seventeen.

She had a carefree and happy childhood, perhaps overly loved by her parents, and especially indulged by her father. The girl was naughty and innocent at the same time. She was so well protected she had no idea that life could be difficult. Because she had been indulged, she was also somewhat bossy.

Tieling's Chess Club had a similar layout to that of the Plum Valley chess school where he studied with his master. It had a big courtyard in the middle of the buildings, with a large pond. Fat, lazy carp, with long whiskers languidly meandered between water lilies in search of their next morsal. The pond was surrounded by different flowers that blossomed in different seasons. Spring offered yellow primroses to sing the first spring song. Of course, wintersweet plums would be in full bloom in this season, and the courtyard was full of sweet fragrance. In the summer, the thick green leaves of tall trees gave deep shade from the heat. Autumn air carried the sweet fragrance of Osmanthus. There was a legend that the Osmanthus tree was the image one could see on the moon.

Xiaomei grew up in this courtyard of different colours. She marvelled at the late spring clouds of catkins, carried by the breeze only to drop to the ground, as if forming a carpet of snow.

Winter though, was her favourite season. She loved watching the snow gently float down from above. Especially when it stopped snowing and the snow lingered on tree branches as if everything were crystallised. Usually, Jin Xiaomei would collect snow from the plum flower petals, place them in a jar and bury them underground. According to the *Tea Classics*, the best water for tea was from the mountainside, the second best from rivers. The least desired was from a well. But if people collected snow in a jar, took it out the following summer and used it to make tea, that would be the most refreshing cup of tea.

Often, she would pick a winter flower and place it in a vase in her room to enhance the simple beauty of the furniture.

As a young girl, she loved to feed the carp and often thought how similar they were to wise old men, with their long whiskers. Her least favourite job was tending to the vegetable garden, and so she often shirked that duty.

Chess had been part of her life for as long as she could remember. Although she was not allowed to play, she absorbed the spirit of the game as if by osmosis. As she got older and understood more, she became obsessed with the game. She intuited that there was a secret hidden in each chess piece. As she helped in the club, she surreptitiously paid attention to each game when she served the guests, often following the matches and silently competing in several games at a time, mentally playing both sides of the board. Yet her father refused to teach her. He preferred her to grow up innocently, rather than get involved in the competitive world of men where gambling was a regular practice. What was more, he did not want his daughter to play chess with men, as in the Ming dynasty, the moral and ethical code forbade women from doing so.

Xiaomei often shuddered with frustration, but quickly brought herself under control as she knew it was useless to confront her father directly. Undeterred, she seized an old wooden chessboard that had been discarded in the yard and carried it into her room. She loved the scent of the mahogany wood from which it was made. Xiaomei also enjoyed reading and would burn sandalwood sticks in her room as she read her father's books. She would sneak them out, one at a time, voraciously consuming all her father's military books, as well the classics.

Xiaomei was fortunate enough to inherit her mother's beauty, but her character was totally different from that of her mother's. She was proud and vivacious. Tieling considered his daughter a little unusual. Each time he scolded the girl when she did something wrong, Xiaomei just lowered her head in obedience, and stayed silent, while her eyes shone mischievously, as she thought of something else, not paying attention to her father. Tieling knew that she was a complicated girl, who devoted most of her time to reading his historical books, classics, and other literature. Sometimes, she could be naughty like a boy. She would climb trees, gamble with her father's disciples, and laugh aloud when someone told her a funny joke. All these things were considered unladylike.

Xiaomei eyes were large and expressive, and shone with intelligence. Her nose was straight, adding to the beauty of her face. She was tall and slender, walking with her chin up, as if she looked down on others, but in fact she did not as she had a generous character. However, whenever she would ask someone a favour in return, she did so in a business-like manner. Such unwomanly behaviour perplexed her friends, who found it difficult to understand her.

Xiaomei could not understand why her father refused to teach her chess. She observed her father's disciples, who had the utmost respect for him. She loved the chatter, and the sound of a chess piece when it was dropped. Xiaomei longed to be a heroine, and to fight on the battlefield too, if not a real one, then at least on the chessboard.

Upon reaching her seventeenth year, she began to worry about her receding looks, the way every mature woman did. Having read so many historical books, she was fully aware of the way women were discarded or downgraded when the blossoming flower of their youth began to wilt. Her father was an exception, refusing to trade her mother in for a younger, pretty-faced virgin just because she aged. Xiaomei knew wisdom, knowledge and strategy could help her to remain in control of an otherwise uncertain future.

Sometimes, Xiaomei hated her father for his ignorance and prejudice — she felt he was an old fool for not allowing her to formally learn chess. Her mother was not any wiser either, always standing firm with her father's decisions without offering an opinion of her own. The more they forbade her, the more disappointed and restless she became. She strongly opposed her parents, until eventually her father shouted at her, and she relented. She realised that it was pointless to fight, so she would bide her time and wait for the right opportunity. She looked at her mother, who often shed tears because of all the quarrelling in the family. Xiaomei felt confused, because it seemed that her mother wanted her to become just like her – washing every day, cleaning, and cooking, with a dull, expressionless face, and without a spark in her eyes. Xiaomei pursed her lips. She considered her mother ordinary and was determined to not turn out like her.

Although disciplined by her father, Xiaomei would not give up so easily and resolved to go to any length necessary to learn. Often, she hid behind the door of the classroom to overhear conversations between her father and his students. It was here that she absorbed the moves and strategies of chess. She found she processed the complicated strategies easily: for example, when an adviser was moved to the top of the palace corner, it would be difficult for a horse to check the king. And when the cannon was fired into the cold valley, it would be difficult to use it to attack again.

Grudgingly, and unhappily, with a thousand reasons not to give up, Xiaomei drew a chessboard on a piece of paper, adding illustrations of the river of Chu Kingdom and the border of the Han dynasty in the middle of the chessboard. Once she had completed her board, she fell into deep reflection as she used little stones as pieces on the chessboard. Xiaomei's sincerity to play and learn touched almost everyone, except her father.

One day, when eavesdropping at the chess classroom door, she heard her father yelling angrily, "Who stole the three silver coins from my pocket? Stand up! Confess!"

Nobody responded. All the disciples lowered their heads, terrified at the prospect of being driven out of the chess club. "Have you forgotten what I taught you? If you want to achieve excellence in chess, you need to be an upright person. You cannot be greedy for money or power; you cannot wait for good fortune to fall upon you as you do nothing! Watch out for the trap under your feet. Fortune only favours those who try. Stealing is a serious crime. If you start stealing small things now, it's the first step towards moral degeneration."

Xiaomei shivered at her father's words, "Fortune only favours those who make an effort." It was as if the words were meant for her. She would not stand by and do nothing. Ever since she was a child, Xiaomei was aware of her father's bouts of temper, seemingly his only fault. Her instincts told her that her father could not continue to treat his disciples this way. He could lose their affections too easily.

Impetuously she opened the door, smiled, and said, "Father, you can be so foolish. It is best to not treat your students in this manner."

"What are you doing here?" Tieling said in a stern voice. "Leave... Now!"

"I was just passing and overheard you shouting." Xiaomei raised her eyebrow in an arch. "It seems that you are a little drunk today, as you have forgotten something important."

"Me? Drunk? What are you talking about? Go to your room! I'll deal with you later."

"I am not here to make trouble. I had a dream yesterday that my father was drunk and put his silver tassels somewhere, but was unable to remember where. And in the dream, it showed that they would reappear in his pocket the next day."

"What nonsense you are talking? Do you want me to beat you?"

Zhang Zheng peeped at Xiaomei furtively, wondering why she was willing to take the blame for him. He was ashamed of himself for his lack of courage. Yet, she, with her back straight, and her eyes shining with determination as she stared her father down, was full of courage. Xiaomei was not scared of her father's bad temper as she was used to it, knowing the best way to deal with it was to be silent. As nobody responded he felt a little embarrassed. Xiaomei grabbed the opportunity, raised her chin to gaze into her father's eyes. She smiled, "Father, I am sure the missing silver coins will reappear." Tieling looked at his daughter in a strange way, seemingly both surprised and amused. He wondered what kind of a trick the girl was up to this time. He was certain that three silver tassels had been stolen, how dare she make such a statement in front of his students? But what could he do? He nodded his head and maintained his composure to save face. With this thought he shook his arm in a gesture of frustration. As he walked out the door he said, "Class is over for the day."

The moment Xiaomei saw her father leave, she too left, without looking back at the students. She did not want them to engage her in conversation. Zhang Zheng watched Xiaomei disappear from his sight. He felt shame, regret, and worry. He marvelled at her audacity, which made him feel even guiltier. *Did she know it was me who took the silver?* he wondered.

Xiaomei had a plan. That night, she secretly changed into male clothing and snuck out of the house. She was excited and scared at the same time. Even though it was a cool night, she was sweating with the anticipation of being caught. She was not sure whether her plan would work, and she could lose the little money she had. But she wanted to test her level of chess ability, and gain an extra three silver coins.

She walked the streets, passing many people. Some were out for a good time, others were hurrying along, getting on with their day. She shivered a little as she walked against the cold night's wind. She finally found a small chess club and went inside. It was warm and noisy, and the air was heavy with sweat and dirt. She stood to one side watching a game in progress. Instinct told her the older man would win. She gave a coin to the owner to bet on him doing so while some of the other onlookers bet for the younger player to win. As the game went on Xiaomei felt her heart in her mouth. It was a thrilling match. She, like the other gamblers, clenched her fists, gesticulating and shouting like the men around her. The older man won, and she received her money back and an extra coin.

The man who lost stood up and left the table, and Xiaomei quickly took his place to play. As the pieces were being replaced, she had to kick herself to see if this was just a dream – here she was, wearing men's clothes, sitting in the company of only men. The old man looked at her and said to the crowd, "Now they send children to play me! Still, your money is as good as any. You do have money boy?" She gave the attendant a coin. It excited her, and she was soon lost in the game and the atmosphere.

On that night, luck favoured her. She won that game and gained two extra coins. Xiaomei felt she had escaped detection long enough and did not want to push her luck. She reasoned that she had got what she came here for. Now she needed to get out, return home, and consider all aspects of the game she played, as well as her opponent.

Heading home though, exhilaration overcame her. At first, she did not realise why. Then it dawned on her: being dressed as a man gave her more freedom than she had ever had. Enjoying her newfound freedom, she meandered across town and mingled for several hours.

Upon arriving home, she quickly changed back into her night attire. Next, she tip-toed into her father's study, fumbling in the darkness for her father's robe and placing the three coins in the pocket. Hearing footsteps approaching, with a thumping heart, knowing it was likely to be her father, she hurried out of the room.

Jin Tieling only saw a shadow leaving his room. He had no doubt as to who it was, and guessed it was related to the lost silver. He scoffed at the thought, but decided not to look into it any further. As a chess master, he had enough patience to wait for the next move.

The next morning, the wind had dropped and the sun shone. The students arrived at the chess club in ones and twos. Over the period of their studies, Xiaomei got to know most of them, and even became friends with some. She followed them into the classroom. Though not allowed in, she sat out of the way in a corner. She smiled at them all. Zhang Zheng was greatly embarrassed, feeling like an ant on a hot pan, he turned his face away from her. He had endured a sleepless night, ridiculing himself as a coward for allowing a girl to take on his burden. With great fear and a lot of inner struggle, Zhang Zheng finally gained his courage. He decided to speak out, "Master!"

Upon hearing Zhang Zheng about to speak, Xiaomei quickly stood up and blurted out, "Father, do you remember what I said yesterday about the three silver coins?"

Tieling frowned, frustrated with his daughter, but nevertheless he nodded his head and waited for her to finish. "Is the money in your pocket?" Tieling's frown deepened. He was unwilling to play this game with his daughter. Nevertheless, he reached into his pocket. When he took his hand out, he was holding three silver coins.

His disciples began to whisper among themselves, wondering how this had happened. Even Tieling himself began to doubt his own judgment. Was he wrong? Did the money fly back into his pocket on its own? Tieling said, "Since the money is back, I'll not make any further inquiries." Tieling looked at his daughter and frowned imperceptibly for a moment. Then he announced, "It's time to have our chess class. But you girl, leave!"

Zhang Zheng was absent-minded the whole day. His thoughts were on Xiaomei. He knew the master had secretly guessed that it was he who had stolen the money. At least that was what he thought, his heart heavy with the guilty conscience of a thief. Again, he blushed. He just could not figure it out how Jin Xiaomei got the money and how she replaced it. At that moment, Zhang Zheng made a secret pledge to protect Jin Xiaomei for the rest of his life.

When the lesson was over, Zhang Zheng looked for Xiaomei everywhere. Finally, he found her sweeping by the pond. As he approached her, she looked up to see who was intruding on her thoughts. He offered a timid smile and indicated he would like to sit with her. She shrugged her shoulders as if to say 'if you must', and they both sat down. His first words were, "How did you do it?"

Xiaomei paid no attention to him and looked at the lotus flowers in the pond. Then, silently, she picked up a stone to draw a pattern on the ground.

"Xiaomei, I made a mistake. It was me who stole the money. You saved me, but I can't stop fretting and thinking about how you managed to get the coins back?"

"Why did you steal the coins?" Xiaomei asked.

"To give them to beggars on the street. My father would not give me money to help them." Zhang Zheng said with embarrassment. "I can give them back to you when I have them."

Xiaomei said nothing but continued scribbling on the ground.

"Xiaomei I am sorry. What I did was wrong, and I will make up for my mistakes. But I would rather jump into the Yellow River than let you to get into trouble for my sake."

"I played chess to win your three coins back." Xiaomei said in a bored voice. But all night she had lain in bed thinking about the thrill of the game and the freedom she had felt roaming the streets in men's clothing. "Actually, I could have won more than three silver coins."

"Oh, good heaven! But how do you know how to make a bet and play chess?"

Xiaomei laughed drily but said nothing.

Zheng felt even more inadequate and was lost for words until Xiaomei burst out laughing, easing the tension, "You look like a clown, frowning."

"Xiaomei, don't be naughty. How could you do something like that?"

"It was just a one-time thing, no harm done." Xiaomei smiled nervously and became quiet again. Zheng sat quietly by her side until she continued, "If you are really grateful to me, there is a way to return the favour."

"I would do anything for you."

"Easy, easy! I will not ask you to steal or kill or do anything immoral. What I ask is quite simple." She put on her sweetest face and asked in her sweetest and most innocent voice, "Please teach me what my father has taught you about chess!"

"Xiaomei, I can only promise that I will protect the *Plum Valley Chess Club* with all my being. But yes, I will teach you."

"Do you promise to keep it a secret, and not tell anyone else?" Zheng nodded his head in loyal obedience.

Xiaomei was delighted. A slight side smile appeared on her face as she anticipated the prospect. Two dimples showed vividly on her cheeks. Zheng stared at her, bewitched.

But later, when Xiaomei was about to enter her room, she was halted by her father's harsh voice. "Stop!" She turned around and smiled sweetly, as if an angel. "What the hell did you do? How did you get the three coins?" he demanded

"I played chess and bet on winning." Xiaomei said matter-of-factly. Hearing this, Tieling slapped her across her face, knocking her back a few steps. "Ouch!" She covered her face with her hands, hissing with the sting. Tears of grief and pain rolled down her face. She wanted to check herself but was unable to do so. Her father roared at her, "Do that again, and I will beat you with my own hands! The worst thing for a chess player to do is to gamble on their chess game. You play for love not for money."

"How dare you blame me? And why are you so cruel to me? Ha-ha-ha, Father, I laugh out of pity for you as all your friends and family fear you. Your disciples, me, even Mother!"

Tieling trembled in anger. He thought that his authority had been challenged. Soon, though, he calmed down a bit and saw that his daughter was right. He was sometimes too belligerent and bad-tempered.

Xiaomei felt her father softening, but she still felt greatly wronged. No one understood her. With this troubled state of mind, she walked away.

In her room, once she had simmered down, Xiaomei reflected on her upbringing. She was content in her father's chess club, living her life without being troubled by worldly conventions. Every day she saw people of all types coming to play chess. It was always loud with the sound of many pieces being stamped on the chessboard. The talking and shouting, mixed with excitement was a kind of tradition to her. Xiaomei smelt the power in each game. She was always watching the games, the guests, the play acting, or intimidation, of a move done well or badly — she took it all in. All had one goal: to win.

She recognised and got to know the better players. She felt sorry for them when they lost. Some were calm and reflective, others chuckled philosophically and made light of it. Some players were too eager to win; if they lost a game, they were devastated. Others were greedy; they played as if they were hunting as opposed to trying to win. The worst were those who were so obsessed with the game that they cared for nothing else. For the sake of chess, they would abandon their family and neglect their work. If they won, they would forget everything, overwhelmed with joy. However, if they lost, their world collapsed. Many had mundane jobs, and playing chess was the excitement they needed to keep them going. Some wanted to climb higher, thinking that chess might be a shortcut, but in the end they only fell into the abyss. Others played to forget the troubled times. There were players who wanted to achieve adulation, only to find out it was an empty wish. One tiny mistake and they would lose the game. Win or lose, they all came for the thrill of the game. The *Plum Valley Chess Club* that was a kaleidoscope, reflecting life in all its diversity, and Xiaomei loved it.

As she reflected, she concluded that playing chess was a gamble, in that you had to change your tactics according to that of your opponent's. Chess was not really about winning or losing, because when playing an opponent, one was really playing oneself. Each move reflected your versatility, your wits, and your focus. If you failed to master these, then you failed yourself. People gambled by placing their wisdom on the chessboard. But she was smart enough to know that losing one game did not mean you would continue lose forever. The same theory worked for winning. She did not know if she won today's game with her father or not.

$$\text{᪣ } \text{᪣ } \text{᪣ } \text{᪣ } \text{᪣ } \text{᪣}$$

One day, Xiaomei tried again. "Father, why won't you let me learn to play chess properly? You know that I know how to play. Give me a chance and you will see for yourself how much I adore the game. Father, you know I am different. I do not want to be a housewife like Mother. Yes, she is happy, but I wouldn't be! I can make you proud of me."

Tieling listened to everything she had to say, and slowly shook his head, "There is no reason. You are just not allowed to learn." He was annoyed by his daughter's persistent demands. And the more she insisted, the more determined he was to ignore her, irrespective of her logic.

Jin Tieling's disciples heard the argument between the Master and his wilful daughter. They flocked to the door to watch. Tieling felt he was losing face, so took her by the hand, and led her to her room, where he locked her in. Xiaomei felt belittled by this. She shouted and kicked the door but in vain.

At noon, Xiaomei's mother came to calm her down. When she opened the door, she saw Xiaomei's face was drawn with frustration and anger. Her eyes were red and swollen like two peach pips. "My child why don't you give up? Is chess more important than your life? You are too stubborn. You must listen to your father, he only thinks of your welfare."

Still Xiaomei would not give up and clutched at the last straw, "Mother, I beg you… Please will you talk to Father? What harm can come to me if I learn chess?"

"No!" Wen's voice was firm.

Why not? was the question that haunted Xiaomei. She stared at the floor in despair. She decided she would defy her parents and use Zhang Zheng to teach her.

Wen continued with an expressionless face, "Your father is always right. You must follow his advice. This is what we women are taught to do."

Of course, Xiaomei was greatly annoyed at hearing these stupid social doctrines, and threw her chopsticks to the floor in fury. She said to her mother stubbornly, "I'd rather starve to death than give up learning chess." Her mother shook her head, said nothing, and walked away silently. She could foresee problems ahead.

Xiaomei was irritated, as her mother's silence hurt her more than her father's scolding or threats to beat her. She did not realise until now just how much she wanted the support of her mother. Listlessly, she passed two days in a state of disillusion. She kept to herself, mostly in her room.

Using the old chessboard and stones she had made, she tried to recall some of the games she had witnessed. She was so focused that at first she did not notice the door opening. Then without looking up, thinking it was either her father or her mother, she sullenly called out, "Leave me alone!"

"My dear lady! What bad manners." A soft and warm voice came to her ears. Xiaomei looked up and saw Zhang Zheng standing by the door, holding hot food in a tin pot. She gave him a wane smile, ashamed and surprised.

"See what I bring you?"

Xiaomei took a look, and saw that it was bird's nest soup, normally one of her favourite meals. "I have no appetite."

"Why not? Look at yourself in the mirror. You look tired, pale and thin."

Xiaomei felt hurt by his words. It was true that she had not eaten much over the past two days. She turned her head away without saying anything.

Zheng sighed, "Are you really so crazy about the game?"

Xiaomei's eyes were filled with tears; all she could do was nod.

Zheng was alarmed to see her so miserable. He wanted to use a handkerchief to wipe the tears from her face, but he dared not touch her.

Still staring at the floor, she tried to put her thoughts into words and murmured, "I will try and explain… it is hard for me to put in words, but I will try. You know when you are outside at night and look up at the brilliant stars, feeling so small, but wonderous? Well that's the feeling I get from chess. And, when in nature, we often feel a sense of grandness because of how it all works together? That's how I feel about chess. Perhaps it is because each game is like a mini life playing out on the board, where we think we have control, but we often don't. Where things don't go as we want. Each game is not a quest to win, but a quest to play it with the best mind-set. Perhaps I am not making sense to you, but this is how I feel for the game. Anyway Zheng, please start to teach me. You promised me you would. Show me what my father taught you."

"Well..."

"You said you were willing to do anything for me. It's not an excessive request, is it?" Zheng felt a pang in his heart. He felt uncertain, as he knew Master would not want him to teach her, but he was too attracted to her to refuse. With her gripping and inspiring words, she had reached a depth within him. He realised that she had put in words what would never come to his mind. "Alright...We will start right now. Well, as soon as you eat this meal I got for us."

CHAPTER FIVE
THE OPENING

Zhang Zheng started by teaching Jin Xiaomei about the opening moves of a game. They met secretly behind the pond. Whenever Zhang Zheng finished the class, he would meet Xiaomei, where he regurgitated the lesson he just received from the Master. He tried to recall every detail. "Your father always emphasises that there are many ways to open a game. The opening is like choosing a military tactic. In ancient times, there were several military strategies deployed on a real battlefield, such as single line battle array, fish scale battle array, full moon battle array... etc."

Some of these were vaguely familiar to Xiaomei from the history and military books she had read. She made a mental note to reread them. Continuing, he said, "So the opening emulates these real military battle arrays... Just imagine you are a general commanding the army, you can either attack from the middle or attack from both flanks. You can end the game quickly or proceed with your war slowly. Sometimes, for the sake of winning the game, you need to sacrifice some pieces to gain the initiative." He drew these military battle arrays on pieces of paper in simple sketches.

Xiaomei felt her pulse pounding. This was amazing. It was her first time seeing these mysterious military battle arrays and tactics drawn out for chess. She had once heard the story of her father's grandmaster Wang Siyi, and she longed to be like him. Her eyes shone with enthusiasm. For the first time in months, Xiaomei was radiant.

Zheng noticed the immediate changes in her when she touched the chess pieces. She was transformed. The spirit of competitiveness pulsed through her body. He could not help but stare at her. So pretty, so clever, so determined, and now glowing. He felt privileged to be a part of her learning and happiness.

Xiaomei smiled and joked at him, "What a funny man you are! Why do you stare at me like that?" Zheng recovered himself, blushed, and continued, "Master once said that he could only teach us chess strategy from the first volume of the book *The Secret under the Mahogany tree*. In other words, our main tactic is to gain the initiative. This is a manual created by Master Wang Siyi. There were two volumes, but I heard that the second volume is kept at the *Happiness Chess Club*."

"What's the difference between gaining the initiative and losing the initiative?"

"I don't know. Master used to say that, logically speaking, they were the same in warfare. Whether gaining or losing initiative, our purpose in playing chess is to win. Have you read the history of what happened in the Spring and Autumn period? In one battle, a king retreated one thousand steps to lose the initiative, but he won the battle eventually. A good chess player can quickly appraise all possible consequences before taking action. You must be broad-minded, fast, and have your wits about you, and you will do well. Anyway, for me, it doesn't matter whether you gain or the lose initiative, as the purpose is to win."

Xiaomei found Zheng's words made sense. She stored them in her memory. "Did my father mention to you why we only have the first volume of *The Secret under the Mahogany tree*?"

"Master once said with much regret that on the night when he left the Valley, his master gave him both volumes of the treatise. But for some reason he gave the second volume to his friend and only retained the first volume. But it seems that the two friends have turned into enemies!"

"Oh." Xiaomei frowned and wondered why her father was so stupid as to have given the second volume of the manual away.

"Have you decided which chess opening you are going to choose for our game?" Zheng asked. Xiaomei frowned and thought a while, "Can you explain a little more about openings?"

"All right, I will repeat. The opening in chess is a model of military battle arrays. For example, if you use your central cannon to charge at the king as the opening tactic, it is equivalent to attacking a city with a big cannon on a real battlefield. However, by doing so, your defence will be weakened. It may be pragmatic to use a screen of horses (two knights) as a defence strategy. Master once told us that you had better not try this central cannon charging as an opening as a beginner unless you are confident and strong. However, it is quite a normal opening for a chess game."

"So, is that your favourite opening?" Xiaomei asked him.

"Yes. The cannon is my favourite weapon, so I like to use a central cannon opening to charge the opponent."

"Hmmm."

Over the following months Zheng continued to teach her how to play chess. He did his best to use the legacy of his master's line. Xiaomei relished the spirit of the tactics. Zheng was a good chess player, but he was nowhere near achieving the status of a master. He was a good teacher though, and remembered everything he had learnt. He was inflexible in his playing style, blindly believed in everything that Master Jin Tieling taught, and never tried out other methods. But Xiaomei instinctively knew good chess players were curious and examined all possibilities.

Xiaomei finally mastered the various different openings, and which ones to use depending on her opponent. With great perception, she determined Zheng's character, strengths, and weaknesses. Zheng was too conservative in his personality, and it was reflected in his game strategy. When they played, he could only check her king after taking all of her pieces. In this way, Xiaomei found that Zheng was a reliable and loyal person. Her respect for him grew.

CHAPTER SIX

THE MASTER OF PLUM VALLEY CHESS CLUB

Autumn turned into winter. It soon became obvious to Xiaomei that she was out-stripping Zheng's knowledge of chess strategy. She had grasped all he taught her and won all their games. At this stage, Xiaomei was improving but still did not have enough focus to play a long game. She found that she would get overwhelmed when her pieces were surrounded by her opponents and panicked as if she was on a real battlefield.

One afternoon, Jin Tieling was playing a game with his friend Tang, and Xiaomei was instructed to serve tea for them. As usual, she scanned the chessboard, seeing that her father's horse was suddenly hobbled by Tang's advisers (a piece in lieu of a queen) and was unable to move to a free square. The game was seemingly in deadlock. Tieling considered his options. Xiaomei should have known the game etiquette better than to comment, but did so without thinking, "Father, in two moves your chariot will be taken by Uncle Tang's cannon."

Tieling was so shocked by his daughter's grasp of the crucial points of the game that he forgot to be angry. He pondered her advice and found it was sound, his chariot was indeed exposed. But then Tieling could not help but feel suspicious. How could she know the lay of the game with just a casual glance? But his thoughts were interrupted by Tang, who quietly observed the dynamic between father and daughter. With a mischievous smile he asked his friend, "Tieling, you always beat me, do you mind if Xiaomei helps me?"

"She can't play chess." Tieling pulled a long face and flatly refused.

"Don't be modest. I think your daughter is a far better player than you think. I have a feeling that she is gifted and will be good if trained properly."

Xiaomei was ready to seize this golden opportunity, "Thank you my dear Uncle Tang. My father refused to teach me, but I can still play a little. At least, I can solve this game." She did not care about her father's scolding her later, all she wanted was to be given a chance.

Tang was amused by this eighteen-year-old girl. Xiaomei smiled, put down the tea tray on a sideboard, and carried another chair over. "Uncle Tang, thank you. Perhaps I can play Father's side?"

Tieling glared at his presumptuous daughter with consternation. Reluctantly, he moved his chair aside so she could sit at his side of the table. As she sat, the adrenalin rushed through her body. At last, she had another opportunity to show her ability in the game. Now playing for her father, it was her move. She studied the board. Although she had seen an opening, she wanted to absorb the game fully. She frowned a little, and then moved her piece, a horse to threaten a cannon.

"Good move!" said Tang encouragingly.

Tieling was flabbergasted, his face gloomy. Yes, the move was clever as it placed the pressure on her opponent.

As the game progressed and he watched Xiaomei play, first securing her pieces, then moving into a dominant position, he could not believe how astute she was. And yet, a feeling of relief washed over him at the same time.

In the end, after a close affair, Xiaomei announced with her typical understated side smile, "Checkmate, Dear Uncle. Thank you for the game." With that she stood up, then kowtowed respectfully first to her father, then to her uncle.

With a gleam in his eye, Tang said, "Indeed, your father has taught you well."

Xiaomei smiled. "But Father never taught me. He refuses, as he thinks a girl cannot play chess."

"Then who taught you, if not your father?" Uncle Tang asked.

"I taught myself. As Father would not teach me, I observed games and listened as players spoke of strategy. I reconstructed games in my room." She said this as she pouted her lips like a spoilt child towards her father.

"Oh, Tieling, my old friend, she has a gift. You can see for yourself. You must teach her how to play. Besides, what harm can it do?"

"Can you give me the name of one woman who can play chess in the current dynasty… or any past dynasty?" Tieling asked with contempt.

"If this is how you really think, I can only say that I feel greatly ashamed of you. We chess players should never be inhibited by social formality and stupid conventions. The very game is about inventiveness. If we find someone who has a gift, and if that person wants to learn, we must explore that talent, even if that person is a girl. You know as well as I do that women are not inferior to men."

Xiaomei wanted to chip in, but considered it best that Uncle Tang do the convincing, so for once she kept quiet.

"So Xiaomei, are you ready to play chess?" Tang asked again.

"Yes, it's been my greatest wish since I was a little girl coming to this club." Xiaomei said with nostalgia. As he spoke, Tang watched Tieling out of the corner of his eye. His friend was no longer looking so belligerent. Then with the coup de gras, he teased his friend, "Well, if you do not take her in hand, then I will teach her... Or worse, someone else will!"

Before Xiaomei could say thank you, her father blurted out, "No, thank you. There is no need... Daughter, if you must learn, I will teach you to play."

With these words, the words that she had waited to hear all her life, a smile of relief broke on her face. But before she could offer her gratitude, her father gruffly interjected, "But there are rules. Now! You will listen."

"Yes, Father. Of course, Father." As she said this, she glanced at Uncle Tang, who gave her a wink of encouragement.

"The next rule is that you always obey and respect me as your master, even if I seem to make a mistake. You are to follow a tradition. For good or bad, I am the custodian of that that tradition. The great master Wang Siyi sacrificed his life for the game of chess. For you to embrace the Wang Siyi tradition, the first thing you must do is become humble, and learn to control your vanity. You are only one pitiful grain of sand on a large beach. Humility, humility, humility."

Xiaomei was overjoyed to now be officially part of the Wang Siyi tradition. Its value warmed her heart.

"First, though," her father said, "do you want to learn, just so you can play for fun? Or do you want to enrol in a life's work, much the same as a devotee would become a Buddhist monk?"

"Father, I have wanted my entire life to be part of this tradition. I can't say where my dedication comes from. But like a Buddhist monk, I have a calling."

"Are you ready to learn discipline and engage in many hours of dreary work?"

"I am."

"And are you ready to embrace the bittersweet feeling that is an inseparable part of learning any discipline?" She nodded her head in solemn agreement. She looked so resolute and steady, he wondered *is this not the discipline and dedication that he sought from his daughter all these years? We will see he thought.* He looked at the light in her eyes. Hardly ever had he seen this in a man. She looked as if she was a bird of prey, ready to capture her prey, dangerous and savage.

That night, after dinner, Tieling told Wen Wen that he was going to teach their daughter the discipline of chess. He was sure he saw a smile light up her eyes.

ꙮ ꙮ ꙮ ꙮ ꙮ ꙮ

Jin Tieling loved his daughter very much, of that there no doubt. He always dreamt of having a child who would follow in his chess footsteps, someone he could teach the Wang Siyi way. Of course, he hoped this would be a boy. When Xiaomei was born, he could not help connecting the child's fate to her mother. He felt pity for them, as a woman's fate was sealed from birth. It had seemed inconceivable to him that a girl would upend this tradition and play chess. Xiaomei had grown up into a pretty but headstrong woman, exacerbated by her quick intellect. She had the fierce dedication required of a potential master or grand master, as well as the requisite compassion and humility.

The greatest achievement of any master was to identify and coach a student of such potential that they surpassed his own knowledge and skill. Seldom did this happen. Now, as Tieling encouraged and disciplined his daughter in the rigour of chess, he wondered if he was going to be one of those lucky masters.

"Tell me," he asked her during her first lesson, "What would you do if you lost a game?" Xiaomei paused, as she had honestly never thought about it. She pondered, "If I lose, I will gain experience and draw lessons from my mistakes." Xiaomei said rather haughtily.

Jin Tieling nodded his head, "What if you win?"

"Isn't winning the goal of the game?"

"Yes, to win is the main aim of playing chess. However, throughout your life, you will not be able to win every time. Life is full of contradictions. There will be occasions when you're riding high, but there will also be times when you're down and losing games by making smalls mistakes. As in life, every chess game is unpredictable. We can never predict our opponent's moves, nor what is going to happen in our life. We try our best, hoping that luck is on our side. Not until the end of the game can you know for sure whether you have won or lost. And even a winner is only as good as his last game. But in life, you can win many times, only to lose in the end. Never take anything for granted, as everything is continuously moving and changing, like yin and yang."

"I understand. I will try my best."

"As a chess player, you need to be ready for any and all hardships that may come. You have told me that you are ready for them and I believe you." For the first time in a long time, her father smiled at her, then continued, "Chess is a paradox. To some it is just a game. To others it's a mission. In the game, each player has his favourite weapon. Some love chariots. Others love the cannon because it is efficient when attacking a city. Then there are those who rely on their horses, as they are flexible. As a rule, at the beginning of the game, it is better to utilise your cannons. You can image that in a real battle, cannons are used to bombard the gate. At the end of the battle, it may have been better to keep the horses. A knight is a flexible piece." He paused for her to take in what he had just said before asking, "In a battle, at the end of the bombardment, what will the soldiers do?"

She thought of the military books she has read and answered, "Pull out their weapons, and engage in close combat."

"Correct! That's why horses or knights are useful and flexible at the end of the game."

She asked, "Does each piece on the board have a specific meaning? For example, does this elephant represent something outside of chess?"

"As you have read my historical books, you should have some idea. What do you think?"

Xiaomei pondered for a while, and said, "I guess the elephant is the same as the ministers of the court. The minister is responsible for making internal affairs decisions for a country. If we want to check the king, it's better to eliminate the opponents' elephant first."

"Yes! If one elephant is taken, the defence will be weak. Now do you see the metaphor between war and chess? A good general is usually a good chess player. But it is not necessarily the case that he is a good general because he is a good chess player!" He went on to relate the story of his master's disciple, Dan Yu, who, because of his chess training and knowledge of military, rose quickly through the ranks of the emperor's army. "But that is enough for today. I want you to clean around the pond, with humility, and consider what you have learnt today."

"Yes, Father. Thank you, Father." She gave a quick bow of her head and headed for the courtyard.

The next day, Xiaomei played a game with her father. He was ruthless and quickly conquered most of her pieces. Xiaomei felt panic-stricken and slapped the table in frustration. Her father, standing up to depart, said, "Winning is easy. You must learn how to lose with grace." Gradually, through a thousand failures, guesses and calculations, her focus deepened. She learned to control her emotions and remain clearheaded even when losing.

Some three months after Xiaomei started her lessons, Tieling felt she was ready to take the next step. "I have the first volume of *The Secret under the Mahogany tree* in my hands. This is half of the life's work of Grand Master Wang Siyi. It is an heirloom of untold riches. My master gave this to me before he disappeared into a life of solitude." As he spoke, the girl reverently turned over each page. Her hands trembled. She saw the Chinese characters on the book cover, *The Secret under the Mahogany tree volume one.* "The first pages show formulas for beginners. You should study these and keep them in mind. They are the essence of chess. These formulas bear some similarities to the military book by Sun Tzu, *The Art of War.* You should also reread the military books and classical historical books, such as the *I Ching (The Book of Changes).* I know you secretly read all my books. This time you do so with my permission and encouragement."

"Thank you, Master!" Xiaomei, now happy now to adhere to his authority. He was well aware of her respectful use of 'Master'.

Soon after, Zheng dropped by for a visit. He was greatly encouraged by Xiaomei's demeanour. He could tell she was flourishing. "So, what have you learnt?" he asked.

She burst out, childlike with enthusiasm, "Ah chess is warfare, but also a metaphor for life. It is strategy, and knowledge. It is experience, both on and off the chessboard. It is unfailing focus. The opening of the game, the movement of pieces, the strategies, and many other elements, all determined your success or failure. There are many important strategic points on the chessboard for each piece. For example, the 4th, and 6th file are important to a Chariot...."

"Woah, hold up a second Xiaomei. Take a minute to catch your breath."

"Sorry, I get excited. Come, Father has given me a few hours off. Let's go to the river."

❧ ❧ ❧ ❧ ❧ ❧

"Father, why did you ask me how I feel about winning or losing before I started my lessons? Isn't it normal for a chess player to win or lose a game?"

"I asked you because I want you to be better prepared. You haven't played chess with many other people yet. You don't know how captivating and absorbing a real competitive game is. A person's chess style is especially important, as it reflects their character. All of these must be known to you before you embark on the game."

"I understand." Xiaomei said, feeling nervous. "Is it wrong of me to want to be the best player? To be a sort of heroine?"

He simply said, "It is hard to hit the target if you look in a different direction."

One day, Tieling came to his daughter's room to find her studying the manuscript, looking at formulas. "What a good student," he said to her. "It's easy to learn how to play chess, but quite hard to become an expert. Only by continuous practice and study can you become expert.

"As you have often heard me say, to be a chess player, you need to have high moral standards. Actually, I cannot teach you how to have high moral standards, only you can do that, through your choices and habits. But if I live my life according to high moral precepts, hopefully you will see their value and follow suit."

"Yes, Father. You are a very moral man, as is mother a moral woman. Hopefully, I can emulate you both in action... Father, I have a question. Do great masters remember every game they play, so that they can take control when a similar game occurs?"

The master was pleased with this question, as he could see his daughter had been thinking about the game, "Even within a single chess game there are hundreds of permutations. There is no game like any other. Like faces, no two are the same. However, there are still some rules to follow. In answer to your question, a master remembers many of the strategies that he lost or won by. But as no two games are the same, he must be astute enough to know a game can go any way. So, he must be aware and objective after each move by an opponent. Great masters remember every game they play, but they change their strategy even in similar games. As to the strategies, they are forever changing. But there is a general rule for each beginner. For example, if both players use the central cannon to charge the king as an opening, it is better to move chariots by the riverside earlier (the border of each player's chess territory). If the chariots are moved to the riverside, they are able to drive away other pieces, as chariots can move horizontally and vertically. Then they can eat away at all the pieces which dare cross the border. At the end of the game, if the elephants and the advisers are still alive, they can repel any attack from a horse and a pawn. Two elephants and advisers can force a draw if the opponent only has one chariot left in the end game. If your military forces are strong on the battlefield, you have the potential to win. If your pieces are scattered here and there, without a root, you must parley for peace. Real chess masters are farsighted enough to judge the situation and take preventative measures before it is too late. So, in this way, memory and tactical ability are combined. Does that answer your question?"

"It does, but I must think about it more. Is this written by the Grand Master?"

With reverence he said, "It was written by Wang Siyi the Grand Master, and his favourite disciple, my master, Chong Xu."

"Whose chess skills were more advanced? Grandmaster Wang or your master?" Xiaomei asked with interest.

"Grand Master Wang Siyi was the greatest player of the time. My master Chong Xu was exceptional, but he was not a Grand Master. He was a wonderful teacher."

"Is it wrong of me to want to be a master?"

"Child! It's difficult to become a chess master. Don't think too much about it for now. I only hope that by learning chess you can find your own meaning in life. If you do, you can be called a master too. But it is good to want to be the best you can be."

"Are you a chess master Father?" She asked eagerly.

"No, I am not." Tieling said rather pitifully. "I can only say that I am good at chess, but I am not a genius. Chess geniuses are rare, like a snowflake that does not melt when held. Perhaps you will achieve more than I have or will. You are more gifted."

Xiaomei nodded her head, "Father, I will try my hardest."

CHAPTER SEVEN
JIN XIAOMEI LEARNS

Not wanting a girl to disrupt his main class, Jin Tieling taught Xiaomei on her own in private sessions. He was strict with his daughter when giving lessons, even a little overly hard on her. He would often punish her by his pointing stick if she made a mistake. Yet Xiaomei never resented her father's punishment, and instead would castigate herself for the mistake. *Father was right!*

"If you want to match the best, you needed to use your brains." Xiaomei would clench her jaw and try harder. Her father spurred her on and encouraged her not to give up.

It was at this time that Xiaomei started to have greater fluency in her game. She had long since moved past the clumsy stage of learning the value of each piece. Whenever she played, she felt like she was transported to a real, brutal battlefield — the rising yellow sand aroused by the galloping of horses, armour shining on the soldiers' backs, pointed sticks buried in the ground, the beating drums and sounding of horns. She felt herself a soldier — a warrior, or a general — fighting a battle for life and death. When her pieces were surrounded by opponents, she felt uncomfortable, as if she were choking.

During one lesson, her father said to her, "Sometimes you need to be hard. It is like when I shout at you. In the end it is best for your game. In real war, it is kill or be killed."

Finally, he encouraged her to play chess with other players, on the condition that she dress as a boy. She was thrilled at the prospect. She was eager to win, and to measure her ability. The other students were surprised at Jin Xiaomei's progress. In the beginning, none of them took her seriously. But it did not take long before they regarded her as a dangerous opponent. Her father taught her various openings, for example a Cross Palace Cannon. It was a slow attack, with a steady build up strategy. He advised her to hurry to 'fly the elephant (minister)' in the palace to maintain the changes. The central cannon would constantly be on hand to check the king.

Then he spent time on opening with the Middle Pawn. Compared with The Cross Palace Cannon as an opening, the middle Pawn opening was rational and aggressive, and one seldom gained the initiative by choosing this opening. The third opening that she liked was the Angel's Guide, which was also a 5th or 7th pawn opening. This opening offered a 'wait and see attitude' to test the opponent's ability.

When she reached nineteen years of age, with the first leaves falling from the trees as autumn approached, Xiaomei's desire for romance suddenly awakened. Up until this time, seldom did her thoughts go beyond the *Plum Valley Chess Club*. Now that she had become a keen strategist, she imagined what it would be like to meet 'the one', fall in love at first sight, and grow old together. Suddenly, she felt a spasm in her stomach. Yes, of course he must also be a good chess player.

Xiaomei still did many of the cleaning jobs in the club, but it was the cleaning of the beautiful and simple courtyard that gave her pleasure. She was like a child born of the earth. The moment her feet touched the ground of the courtyard she would reenergise. She cultivated the flowers and pruned the trees to make them look neat. It was still her job to feed the fish, and she would not allow anyone else the privilege.

Tieling encouraged his daughter's whim, and he was satisfied at the result of the work. If using a quotation to describe the beauty of the courtyard, we would use a quote from Daoist philosopher Laozi: *Simple is the best. Too much can clutter.*

She longed to visit beyond the city, to see mountains and rambling rivers, as men did. Thus far, she had no chance of travel. Starting from her earliest childhood, her mother would cram her head with rules and standards. She hated it and would find comfort in the poetry from *the Book of Songs*.

In other people's eyes, Xiaomei was unpredictable and complicated. She never played chess dogmatically, but moved pieces fast with accurate calculation. Moreover, people were put-off by her haughty air.

On a cold autumn afternoon, an early snow was falling and the club was nearly empty. Xiaomei and Tieling were to play what they thought would be a relaxed game, but after a considerable battle she won the game. Her father announced with a satisfying laugh, "You have defeated me, good girl!"

Trying to be humble, "So, does it mean that I can play and challenge other recognised players now?"

"Yes." Jin Tieling's eyes were still smiling.

Trying to hide her excitement, she simply said, "Thank you Father. You have given me a great gift." She wanted to give her father a kiss, but he was too reserved for that. She was shocked to hear him say, "It is time we find you a husband." He said this with an air of despair, as if now that he and daughter had become so close he did not want to give her away to another man.

"Father, you must not marry me off without my approval." She said this in a petulant but soft and warm voice.

Avoiding the issue, he asked instead, "What kind of husband do you want?" She blushed as never before had there been a conversation such as this one. After considering for a moment, she realised her past fantasies were just that, fantasies. She shook her head, confused. "It scares me Father. I do want a husband… But you know that I could never have one who bosses me around. Or one who, once I get older, turns his attention to another young girl, and discards me like an old chessboard in the back of the courtyard."

Tieling knew his daughter and had considered these things leading up to this conversation. "You know, if we look for a man who has learnt the art of chess, he is likely to be a man of honour and respect. Perhaps we should look for a man from the chess community?"

She brightened up a little at this prospect, but then an important thought dawned on her, "But Father, will such a man be happy when I always beat him at chess?'

Tieling burst out laughing, "Daughter, you are indeed a treasure. No quarter given by you. We will have a chess tournament, inviting people from all over town. We will suggest that the young men come and take up the challenge." Then with a teasing gleam in his eye. "The winner will become your husband."

Her face was as red as fire. "Father!" she burst out, "How could you?"

Tieling laughed but she continued, "I must be allowed to play in this competition. Whoever becomes my husband must know that chess is important to me. Besides, it will also provide a common love that we can share."

However, at nineteen, this young woman was still full of fantasy. She enjoyed dressing up in front of her copper mirror, to pretend that she was a proud and refined lady. She loved the solitude and privacy of this pretend play. After the chat with her father, she pouted as she thought of the implications. She decided she wanted to find a chess player who would be well-matched with her. She also longed to go about town, to other chess venues and play chess with other competitors. When such an idea occupied her, she was much more excited than she was at the prospect of marriage. And yet she hesitated. Is she good enough to compete with the best outside of the Plum Valley Chess Club? Or was she just a person who had a very narrow view? Would she ever be called a female chess master?

While she was deep in thought, there was a knock on her door. "Enter", she called. Zhang Zheng poked his nose around the door, "Guess who?" he said with a childish giggle. As he came in he was startled to silence. Zheng had never seen Xiaomei dressed up like a lady. He just stood, like a scarecrow out in the fields. He felt clumsy and inadequate; her beauty was peerless. All he could hear was his heart pounding in his ears. "Zheng! What's the matter? You look like you have seen a ghost." At her words he quickly composed himself, "Me… no, of course not. I just came to say hello and share some steamed dumplings. They are still hot," he said lamely.

"That's very good of you. Thank you." Xiaomei took the spare chopsticks and plucked one of the dumplings. As she bit into it, steam escaped. It was filled with three ingredients, shrimp, pork, and chives. It was so tasty that she ate too fast, totally forgetting her manners. Still chewing, she said with embarrassment, "Sorry, I must be an awful sight. I'm so hungry. This dumpling is heavenly!"

"What a glutton you are!" Zheng felt all the world was singing just because Xiaomei liked something he'd given her. She wiped a grain of meat from the corner of her mouth cheekily and laughed with pretend gentility.

"Xiaomei, I could never think you are an awful sight." Then in a shy and awkward manner, he stammered out the next sentence. "I wonder if one day I may have the honour of asking you to marry me."

Xiaomei was so surprised by his announcement that she nearly dropped her second dumpling. Never did it occur to her that he would be anything but a friend.

"What! What are you saying? I… I thank you…But I've always thought of you like a brother. I never thought of you any other way…" Then she waved her hands, annoyed, signalling that she did not want to discuss the issue any further.

"My dear Xiaomei. Listen… If we married, we would have good prospects. My father is wealthy, and I will inherit his estate and lands. I wish for us to grow old together." Zheng said warmly.

"Stop, my brother. Stop! For some things it is better that they never be spoken out loud. Otherwise, we can be friends no more."

Zheng was stunned. He had long believed that Xiao-mei would never fall in love with him, but now it was clear. Downcast, he backed out of the room, the dumplings forgotten on the table. He remembered the promise made to her. He vowed that he would still protect her all his life, even if she could not love him. Jin Xiaomei was like a rose that grew in the fertile soil of his mind, the most secret and romantic place in Zhang Zheng's world.

And, as for Xiaomei, she was so confused that she had been rude to him out of uncertainty.

CHAPTER EIGHT
HAPPINESS CHESS CLUB

Under the guidance of her father, Xiaomei studied *The Book of Changes* to enhance her chess ability. He told her that the strategy of chess is ever-changing, and that instead of rigidly following chess theories, she should apply such theories with flexibility. The ancient text espoused: *the changes proceed in daily life and in people's behaviour. Everything looks stable and still in everyday life, while change never ceases.*

Xiaomei was an apt student. She tried to understand the 'change' in a chess game. Each choice could improve or reduce the initiative. One wrong choice, a single bad judgment, could mean the wheel of fortune turns against you. If you acted impulsively and became restless, most moves will lead to your demise.

The ever-changing nature of a game also meant that was useless to memorise chess manuals. Instead, one should play different opponents with different tactics. Even the treasured manual *The Secret under the Mahogany tree,* should be studied well, not followed dogmatically. Xiaomei was never a slave to dogma. Her style was free and flexible, the qualities of a good player.

As Xiaomei was so pretty, Zheng was not the only one who had a crush on her. In fact, just about all the young men in the club did. They discussed her all too often amongst themselves to a point that Tieling could not avoid it any longer. He may have been a good chess strategist, but when it came to his daughter, he a was a novice. One evening after Xiaomei went to her room, he complained about it to his wife, "Just as I thought. She's too pretty and is causing too much of a stir when she enters the classroom. There could be trouble." It was just as well that he did not know of one of his favourite students Zheng's bumbled proposal.

Xiaomei was aware of the admiration of the men at the chess club and derived a sense of impish joy from it. She did not let it affect her too much, as she knew that tomorrow she would be yesterday's girl. Besides, chess held a more important place for her than any man's affections.

One warm afternoon, after her lessons, Xiaomei snuck out of the club to find a private spot to sit by a small lake close to the crowded capital centre. That day, the water glistened like sparkling diamonds as the ripples caught the sun. Xiaomei had loved this lake ever since she was a child. Now, she lay on a blanket by the lake with her arms stretched out wide, looking up through the gently waving elms to see the patches of blue sky. She was relaxed and enjoyed the stillness as her thoughts wandered aimlessly. Slowly, she began to think about what she had read. In *The Book of Changes*, she learnt of animism and wondered if everything in the universe had a soul. Every flower, every blade of grass, every cloud... All had some intelligence of some kind. Though she had not visited mountains and rural areas, her small cosy world was enough for her to ponder her thoughts and theories on animism.

Later, after looking around to ensure she was alone, she removed her socks and shoes, and happily splashed at the water's edge, her bare feet sliding through the muddy bottom. She felt gratitude to God and the ancestors for this simple time. She did not lack food nor shelter, and she had grown up without worries. She was thankful for her father, that he was a skilled chess player chess, and that he had now decided to share his skill with her. Life was peaceful and happy. Then, as often happens with young adults, a sudden well of uncertainty spang up from nowhere. Would she be able to achieve her dreams and ambitions? Was she ever likely to become a chess master in this male dominated world? If she could not, what would that mean for her life?

Her thoughts were interrupted by a splash behind her. She quickly turned around, thinking a fish had jumped up. As she searched the widening ripples to find the source, another splash occurred behind her. Again, she spun around. Perplexed, not seeing any signs of a fish, she heard a muffled laugh. Looking up, she saw Zhang Zheng cheekily grinning with a stone in his hand. He could not resist and let it fly up so high that it came down with a loud plop that splashed her face. Spontaneously, she burst out laughing. He could not stop his mirth.

"Oh, it's you. How sneaky you are!" she said whilst still laughing. As she started to step out of the lake, she realised he was staring at her bare feet. She blushed and cried out, "Ah, turn your back."

Zheng meekly obeyed. He now was embarrassed for having been caught in impropriety.

Xiaomei hurried to put on her footwear. When done, sweetly she said, "You can turn around now." He did so, and she pull a long face and said hurriedly, "First you splash me, then you look at my bare feet. What sort of a man are you?" and then they both burst out laughing. "And why are you stalking me?"

He thought quickly, "Aha, to protect you! Although you are a brilliant chess player, you can't fight with a strong highway man. A girl as beautiful and charming as you will attract the attention of bad people, who are like leopards." The truth was that he also liked this park and was strolling through it when he saw her wading.

She continued the banter, "I am a soldier enough. I do not need a man to protect me."

"On the chessboard maybe but not in real life."

Xiaomei knew he was right and lowered her head shyly. She started playing with grass blades absentmindedly, then equally absentmindedly said, "How weak and soft these blades of grass are!" She used her fingers to bend the grass, "They change their position with the direction of the wind. Do you think grass has a soul?"

"What do you mean?"

But Xiaomei quickly changed the subject, blurting out, "I am extremely vexed that my parents want to marry me off. They discuss it almost every day, like I am a pig to sell. The atmosphere of home is suffocating. That's why I came to this secluded place, for a moment of solitude."

Zheng's face betrayed his confusion at receiving this information. He wanted to say, "Then marry me," but restrained himself. Finally, he summoned his courage and asked, "Among all your acquaintances, do you have a man in mind?" He held his breath as she replied.

"We grew up together since we were children, that's why I can't accept a proposal from any of you. We are too familiar with each other. It's better to be friends, rather than lovers. Oh, Zheng, may I ask you a question?"

"Of course, any question you want."

"You say you want to marry me. Is it not because of some male vanity?"

"All of us in the club adore you wholeheartedly, there is no vanity in it. We are prepared to give up playing chess and go to a real battlefield just to see you smile." he said honestly.

"Oh. Don't say that." Xiaomei frowned, a little disturbed, and quickly changed the subject. She gave him a charming smile, "Let's have a formal competition. The previous ones don't count. Whoever beats me will win me in marriage if they so desire." Neither she nor he could determine the seriousness of her challenge.

Nevertheless, Xiaomei's words spread through the *Plum Valley Chess Club* faster than fire through dry hay. Soon, everyone was talking about the competition to win her hand in marriage.

Eventually, it reached Jin Tieling's ears. Hearing what his daughter had started, initially he was angry that Xiaomei had boldly announced the way she would choose her husband in public, and in such a way. However, he had to acknowledge that she was unlikely to lose, and so the threat of marriage was not likely. Yet, it would continue the tradition of the chess fraternity, just as Wang Siyi's daughter married Dan Yu after Dan Yu won the chess contest in the Plum Valley.

As for Xiaomei, she played a game against all the young men of the chess club. There were even a few others who came to try their luck who were not members of the club. Although she enjoyed the competition, she beat them all with ease. In some games, she teased her opponent by prolonging the checkmate, or by creating handicaps for herself by sacrificing pieces. Sometimes, Xiaomei attacked fiercely and aggressively like a female tiger, playing with strategy. In some games she was bored, and so ended the game quickly. All the young men were downcast, frustrated that they were beaten by a girl. Jin Tieling's students marvelled at her adroitness.

Tieling stood by, watching every game, feeling satisfied. He was proud of his daughter, who seemed to have mastered all the strategies from the manual.

Jin Xiaomei's reputation as a player spread. However, who would have predicted that these happy times would sow the seeds of disaster for the *Plum Valley Chess Club*?

One of Tieling's disciples, Rou Rou, was the son of Rou Zengnan, the master of *The Talented Chess Club*. He, if you remember, was one of the students Wang Siyi had dismissed. Rou Rou, the son, was beaten easily by Xiaomei and was incensed to have been beaten by a girl. After the game, he saw Xiaomei chatting with Zhang Zheng, and strolled over to eavesdrop on their conversation. He hid around the corner of the building as they chatted, and pretended to read a manual while he listened.

Rou Rou had been placed in *The Plum Valley Chess Club* by his father as a spy to report on the club and the people in it. Rou Rou appeared to be a silent man, overshadowed by his father. In fact, he was so shy that he often seemed invisible. Yet he was a shrewd and calculating young man, every bit his father's son. Rou Rou's main task was to find the whereabouts of the manual *The Secret under the Mahogany tree*. For three years, Rou Rou had befriended everyone in the club, and was now beyond suspicion. Over time, he had also reported to his father about the progress of Jin Xiaomei. Now, Ron Zengnan was sure that she had mastered the secrets of the chess manual, and he figured that the treatise must be in her possession. It was an exciting moment for him to consider that the manual could soon be in his grasp.

"Congratulations, Xiaomei! You have defeated us all!" said Zheng, pretending to be depressed.

"Thanks Zheng." Xiaomei said, lapsing into silence.

"What's the matter?" he asked with his usual care.

"I don't know. I just feel low." she sighed.

"The reason you feel down is because you are the winner. The winner always stands alone – when you are on the top of the mountain, enjoying the view, you don't feel the chill of the wind. You are lucky and I am envious. I am so passionate about chess, but I do not have your gift."

"Maybe I don't either. I still have so much to learn." She then asked him, "Do you think our chess club is the best in the capital?"

Zheng hesitated, "Well, yes and no."

"Tell me."

"There are many clubs in the city, but only two stand out because they were disciples of Wang Siyi of the legendary Plum Valley line. The other club is the *Happiness Chess Club*. You know about it because of their master and your father's story. It is *The Secret under the Mahogany tree* that made them both successful, as well as their early lessons. And talking about *The Secret under the Mahogany tree*."

Rou Rou became particularly attentive at the mention of

the manual. They were too engaged in the conversation to notice his shadow on the corner of the building.

"In the previous game, you used tactics that we've never seen before. Were these from that manual? Or did Master show them to you?"

"Yes, they were from the manual." Xiaomei laughed shyly, "from the first volume, showing how to gain the initiative." She then said, "If one chess club was able to obtain both volumes of *The Secret under the Mahogany tree* then there would no match for them anywhere right?" Xiaomei asked excitingly.

"Maybe so, maybe not. We are never likely to know as neither club will willingly give up their volume."

Xiaomei's mind ran fast. She had a premonition that maybe one day she would have a chance to see the second volume. She smiled at the prospect. Xiaomei, with that half side smile asked, *Interesting! If the two chess clubs held a competition, one using the tactics of gaining the initiative, and the other of losing the initiative, who would be the winner?* This idea made her restless with anticipation.

Zheng had been speaking for a while, but Xiaomei was so engrossed with her own thoughts that she barely heard what he was saying until she zoned back in, "... yes Wang Wengfeng has friends in high places. Apparently he is even friendly with the Prime Minister. His wife is from a famous family line. He has a son. Some say he is very intelligent, but I have not met him. There is a rumour that the son is or was engaged to the prime minister's daughter... They also say that Wang Wengfeng is known to be a dark and sinister person, smooth talking but dangerous." "That's horrible." Xiaomei said. Suddenly, she felt a shiver of excitement. She would visit the *Happiness Chess Club* tonight, and if possible, play there and see what transpired. There is a teaching in *The Art of War* that states "Battles can only be won if we know our enemy." She excused herself and hurried back to her room.

"Where are you going?" Zheng asked but she was too preoccupied to hear him.

Rou Rou heard the entire conversation, *So the manuals are real. I must get this book for Father. For once he will be pleased with me. The wheel of fortune has turned in my favour.*

Rou Rou's father, Rou Zengnan, once told his son there was a code in the book *The Secret under the Mahogany tree* that led to a treasure. He had heard a private conversation between Wang Siyi and Chong Xu, and had determined that it was better to treat it as truth. For this reason, he planted his son in *The Plum Valley Chess Club* to determine its whereabouts. The legend goes that after the chess game with Wang Siyi, the emperor Zhu Yuanzhang once tried to find out where the treasure was hidden, but in vain.

So, those who got their hands on the whole manual would not only become the master of chess, but also the richest person in the Ming dynasty.

Rou Rou stalked Xiaomei. When she closed the door to her room, she hurried to dress up as a boy, intending to go out. Rou Rou hid himself behind a column and waited. He then poked a hole in the window paper and looked in. He saw her dressed as a man and wondered why. When she left, he slipped into the room and glanced around, wondering where the volume could be hidden. He rummaged cupboards but found nothing. Then he remembered that Xiaomei took a last look at her make-up case before she left. *Perhaps it's in there.*

Rou Rou opened the make-up case. His hands were trembling as he looked inside. It was messy with a mix of rogue, flower powder, hairpins, and a flower for the hair. It had a strong smell of mixed fragrances. Rou Rou quickly removed these items and finally found a book-like object, wrapped in silk at the base of the box. He took it out, undid the ribbons, and removed the silk protection. It was a book. The name on the book was *The Secret under the Mahogany tree. That's it!* Rou Rou was exhilarated. With his heart pounding he left the room and the premises to return to his father's house.

CHAPTER NINE
THE FIRST CHESS GAME

Xiaomei had always longed for adventure, and now she had one. As she found herself walking along the busy streets, across town to the wealthier section, she mingled with the dense crowds, passing herbal shops, tea houses, biscuit shops, and hostels. Everywhere there were carts selling every food and item imaginable. Occasionally, she stopped someone to ask for directions to the *Happiness Chess Club*. One man told her to look for two large red lanterns. She had to change directions several times, but finally she saw two big red lanterns ahead. As she approached, she saw the sign hanging above a big ornate gate, *Happiness Chess Club*.

The club's frontage was palatial. Her father's club seemed shabby in comparison. She gave a scoffing gesture at the offensive name, pondering whether this chess club had a false reputation. Without a moment's hesitation, she passed a guard and entered the grounds.

She found herself on a zigzagging path that meandered through vibrant and colourful gardens. She passed a pond that made her pond at home look like a puddle. It was full of lotus flowers and regally floating geese, like sailing junks on a harbour. In the middle of the pond was a man-made island with gorgeous flowers of different varieties and many squabbling ducks. Even under the shadow of the trees grew grass and flowers whose names were unknown to her. These were being tended to by gardeners, all of whom were wearing a kind of uniform which had the same colours as the front of *Happiness Chess Club* building. The sweet scent made her feel a little dizzy. She picked up the pace, keen to get inside to play chess.

Eventually she reached a two-story building with balconies wrapping around each floor. Its curved roof and corners projected abundance and softness. The top floor was beautifully embellished with images from nature, painted pine trees and a crane image on the roof. There were five red lanterns on the second floor. Xiaomei entered the building and passed another watchman, who seemed not to notice her. Inside was extravagantly furnished. Xiaomei regarded the decor too lavish for a simple chess club, but later she saw a restaurant, tearoom, and other private areas, which suggested that businessmen held meetings here. Xiaomei observed the guests. All seemed to be of high-ranking officials or business people, all dressed in elegant and graceful silk gowns. She was conscious of being dressed well below their standards of elegance. However, she did not lower her head, and kept her back straight. She recalled what Zheng had said about its owner and his connections. She also remembered what he said about the underhandedness of the dealings that went on there.

She walked past a stage where an old man and a young lady were singing an opera about a familiar cultural story. The old man wanted the young lady as his concubine, but she refused as she loved a young man from her village. In the end she committed suicide rather than be forced to marry him.

She entered a tea house, pausing to find some refreshment and observe the room before she went to find a game. The scene excited and appalled her at the same time. She paid particular attention to the main chess pavilion, to familiarise herself with how it worked for the players. Each chess table was made of high-quality mahogany, with *Happiness Chess club* etched in carved script into the edge of the table. She marvelled at the wealth of the club master. But she was a young girl with courage and insight; this splendour did not deter her. Her sense of dignity and confidence was strong. She was happy with the simplicity that her father lived by. Finishing her tea, she was finally ready and headed towards the pavilion where a blue curtain hung on the door. Above the lintel was a couplet, with the following inscribed: *To see a world in a flower, and enlightenment of Buddhahood in one leaf.*

As she strolled by each table, she consciously took-in each game and the players. At this moment a handsome young gentleman entered the room. He happened to notice the concentration on Jin Xiaomei's face and was intrigued enough to approached her. "Good afternoon sir," he said with confidence and politeness. "You must be new here, I have never seen you here before. Oh, excuse my manners. My name is Wang Jing. My father, Mr Wang Wengfeng, is the proprietor of this establishment." He appraised the newcomer. He noticed the clean but lower-class cut of material of Xiaomei's clothes. She was momentarily surprised to confront one of her adversaries so quickly. She saw that although he was born with a silver spoon in his mouth, he did not seem spoiled. He wore a neat blue coloured brocade silk gown, overshadowing all the other young men in the pavilion.

Still appraising what he thought was a very young, fresh faced man of good upbringing, but from a lower level of society, Wang Jin wondered, *who is this guest? He may be only a young boy, but he is astutely observing everything.*

"Excuse me, sir?" He continued. "Are you here to play chess? You have the look of a fine player. Unfortunately, the tables are full today. You are welcome to try again... Perhaps tomorrow."

"Tomorrow? I have no time tomorrow. No, I will leave. Besides, I see no player of expertise. It was a mistake to come here." She said this with authority, intending to play him as she would play a game of chess. Her first move was to provoke him. "Thank you, but I shall seek a game in another establishment. One of higher calibre."

"My goodness... Young man, how can you be so arrogant before you prove yourself worthy?" Wang Jing said, trying his best to remain in good humour. "You are in the finest club in all the dynasty. Just look around you and see for yourself."

Her second move, with a raised eyebrow, "Does opulence make for chess skill? Or perhaps you merely consider me a country bumpkin of little worth, and not worthy of a table?" With that, she pretended to turn, as if to leave. Her challenge hit home. He was shocked by this young man's insulting manner. He would teach him a lesson and throw his arrogance back in his face.

Wang Jing returned his smile, ready to play *his* first move, "Hold on sir. I'm sure I can organise a table for you. In fact, to give you the best service in the house, I shall take the time and play you myself. Would that be to your liking?"

As she looked at him, her quick mind assessed the situation: *he is the son of The Happiness Chess Club owner. Like me, he grew up with chess all around him. He is likely to be good, very good.*

And now he is like an angry wounded tiger. There is every reason to believe that he has studied his father's portion of The Secret under the Mahogany tree. It seems that her conversation with Zheng earlier was occurring; one of them would be using the tactics of gaining the initiative, and the other of losing the initiative. *He will play with a belief in his abilities, which he will have. But I have the added advantage of surprise, as he knows nothing of my abilities. This may make him less cautious, going for a quick kill, so as to show me my place in the social strata.*

She pretended to study him for a second, "Please do not put yourself out. Someone of your stature playing with a poor boy such as myself…"

His words were smooth, "It is no problem I can assure you." He was not letting this upstart off the hook. "Please follow me."

She nodded in acquiesce and followed him. She was excited beyond belief, but did not show it on her face. If anything, she looked bored. Jin Xiaomei followed Wang Jing through the main playing hall. Many of the players looked up curiously at Xiaomei. He led her into a private parlour that was elegantly furnished. Surrounding the wall were bookshelves filled with hundreds of books, and in the middle of the room was a table which supported a large chessboard. Instantly, she saw that the pieces were made of sandalwood. The fragrance of the wood filled the room with a light essence. She felt a little awkward at the richness of the club. As they sat Wang Jing politely asked, "What is your name?"

"Jin Li!" she quickly responded.

Jin Li, he thought, and tried to decipher his background – *the name is a common one and he was unable to gain advantage there.* "I am pleased to meet you Mr Jin Li.

"As the guest, I invite you to have the first move." She looked him in the eye and nodded her agreement. It was his way of assessing her opening, bold or cautious. Xiaomei choose the red-coloured pieces and made her first move.

She chose a cautious opening with the cross-palace cannon. It was easy to attack and defend at the same time.

Wang Jing recognised the cautious move and smiled inwardly. He felt that this meant his guest was not so confident. He chose the central cannon as his counter to attack Xiaomei's troops in the middle.

Xiaomei decided to gather her forces to Wang Jing's left side. She quickly moved the chariot to the left side of her river in order to force his pieces back. She decided to move the central cannon to strengthen her attack. He in turn moved his two horses to form a strong defence.

As the game continued, tension mounted, both sensing it in the other the determination to win. Xiaomei suddenly attacked Wang Jing head on with her horse, while in the next move she used her central cannon to check. This surprised Wang Jing, who had judged that 'he' was not strong in the offensive. Wang Jing realised that his opponent wanted to win by setting a trap for him, so he decided to retaliate with aggression. He moved his horse to overpower Xiaomei's cannon and continued moving his chariot forward to destroy Xiaomei's pawns one by one. Xiaomei had to defend wave after wave battering the coast. She was feeling slightly overwhelmed, even breathless. She knew she had to change her strategy. She had six pieces left: two elephants, two advisers, a chariot, and the king. Wang Jing had seven pieces: his two elephants, two advisers, one horse, a cannon, and the king. The end game was evenly poised. Their tactics were equally matched. Wang Jing was calculating and played with valour, and Xiaomei could not help but feel the pressure. To play well at this point would mean nothing if she lost in the end — there are no prizes for coming second in chess. The winner gets all the glory. She decided to do something to disrupt his attention, and started to quietly hum a few lyrics from the Chinese opera *The Peony Pavilion*. He tried to ignore it, but it got to him. He fidgeted and was less focused. She observed this, whilst seemingly studying the board.

Instead of focusing on the game, his mind wandered, *why is this boy humming this song at this moment?* This was the first time in his career that he had played such a well-matched opponent. The boy in front of him looked naive, but in fact he was calculating and sly. He was so agitated he decided to speak, "Li, please stop singing? I know it comes from the opera *The Peony Pavilion*, and it is lovely, but now is not the time."

"Sorry, I didn't realise I was singing, I am just enjoying this game so much. Yes, of course I'll stop." As she said this, she moved a high chariot to safeguard her cannon. She was full of whimsical ideas and continued talking, as if to an old friend, "It is my favourite opera. What impresses me most is that the couple love each other, even though the heroine is a ghost." She continued rambling for a few more sentences, finishing up with, "Don't you think true love is difficult to find?"

"Ha-hah." This was his first time hearing a boy, a country boy at that, offering such an eloquent description about *The Peony Pavilion* opera. He realised that the humming and discussion was a ruse to distract him. He had become distracted, and so offered the same in return, "You are a fair player, but I always prevail." He said as he successfully took one of her horses. He continued blabbering. "What's say you and I become friends?" Xiaomei saw the move but was not concerned, replying, "Friends… I don't think you and I could ever be friends. But it is an honour to play with you. After all, we can play chess with our enemies, can we not?" Xiaomei said this with irony as her central cannon exploded into a major initiative that changed the odds in her favour.

Seeing this, Wang Jing focused. Was it too late to repair the damage? Continuing to try and disrupt her, he said in a calm voice, "There are many positive love stories in our long history, such as the famous love between Si Ma Xiangru and Zhuo Wenjun. As for me, I only want to encounter such an honest love as theirs was. To have our hair grow grey together."

Jin Xiaomei felt a pang in her heart. Now it was her turn to be distracted. These were the kind of words that she dreamed of hearing. She knew well the story of Si Ma Xiangru and Zhuo Wenjun and their eternal love for each other. Her eyes softened and she quickly took a glance at him whilst he vanquished her chariot on the riverside, and announced, "Stalemate."

Xiaomei felt she had let herself down, being deceived by the same method she had used on him. She scanned the board for a way to continue. There was none, neither player could move. How foolish of her to allow a stalemate. It showed a weakness in her strategy. Yet, her smile showed conciliation, and a natural disappointment at not winning. Behind the smile, she was furious with herself. "Indeed, it is. Well played."

Wang Jing, equally annoyed with himself, stood, and bowed deeply, "We are well matched in the game. Brother Li, thank you."

Xiaomei did not know what the rivalry between his and her father was, and as she considered this, she did not notice his sincere gesture of friendship. She forced a smile to her face, but said generously, "It was a pleasure. I thank you as well." The words were stiff in her mouth. It was hard for her to admit her failure, and her hands were trembling as she continued. "I must be going. Goodbye, and thank you again." As she started to pass him, Jing clutched her sleeve to delay her, and asked, "Brother Li, will you come to play again? After all, we must have a winner next time."

Xiaomei was a little surprised. She looked at Wang Jing, and thought he seemed sincere. She felt panic in her mind, and just nodded *yes* as she passed him.

Outside, the curtain of night was descending. The clouds were tinted red by the sunset, with dark colours on their edge. She hurried home as she had been away too long.

CHAPTER TEN

THE LOSS OF THE FIRST VOLUME OF THE SECRET UNDER THE MAHOGANY TREE

Jin Xiaomei felt her heart racing on the way home. The emotions that had risen following the stalemate, which to her was like a loss had started to leave her, and she found herself exhilarated. She did not find the street noisy, and enjoyed the people passing by. As she strolled back home, the image of Wang Jing's face came to her. His smile, his gentlemanly manner, and his chess skills replayed over and over again in her mind. She was confused; he was the son of the enemy, he was not meant to be nice.

But after a hint of freedom often comes sadness. When she was back home, Xiaomei found the door of her room open. She always closed it. She wondered if some thief had broken in. Entering the room there was still enough light to see the chaos. Her first instinct was to check if any valuables were missing. As she glanced around, she saw the cupboard was open, though she remembered closing it before she left.

Jin Xiaomei looked for her jewellery and money and found they were all still there. If the thief was not looking for money or treasure, what did he come to her room for? Suddenly, she felt as if she had been punched in the stomach. "No! Not *The Secret under the Mahogany tree?*" Frantically, she scrambled to her makeup box. It was open, the contents unceremoniously discarded on the floor. Her heart skipped a beat, the manual was gone. "Oh, my goodness!" she cried.

Who was the thief? Xiaomei racked her brains, trying to remember with whom she had discussed the manual; the only person was Zhang Zheng. He would never steal the book. Xiaomei thought hard, *If Zheng wanted to learn the contents, he would just ask father or me, and we would have been willing to share the lessons. Besides, he knew the manual was here and would be an obvious suspect. So, if the thief was not Zheng, who?*

Xiaomei closed her eyes, trying to recall every detail of the afternoon. She vaguely remembered a shadow around the corner of the building when she was chatting about the book to Zheng. She forced her memory. The shadow looked thin and tall in her memory. She did not give it a second thought at the time, but now it occurred to her that the person hidden around the corner must have been listening to their conversation. *What did he want that chess book for? To improve his chess skills? No, it was not as simple as that. There must be something more.* Suddenly, Xiaomei was scared and felt very cold. What if her father discovered that the manual had been stolen?

An idea started germinating in her mind. *I could always recreate the book from memory.* She had studied it in such detail that she was sure she could do this. She immediately grabbed paper and brushes to write and draw with and started the process.

While she was writing, she discovered something that she had overlooked before when she had first studied the book. She recalled there was a poem on the cover, but now she realised it only seemed to contain a part of the poem.

> *Of all the chess on the battlefield,*
> *is it a play, or a drama?*
> *If you know how to play with the chess pieces,*
> *you command three armies of military might.*
> *The movement of chariots and horses*
> *traced back to the Zhou dynasty,*
> *other pieces have the title of the advisers of Han nationality.*

It was not a complete poem, so what was the other half? She vaguely remembered the first time she read the poem, she found it a little weird. Some of the characters were highlighted, including battlefield, chariots and horses, and Han dynasty. *Why were these characters highlighted?* Xiaomei dispelled these thoughts and continued reproducing the book as best as her memory allowed. She worked through the night, until finally she fell asleep on the desk.

ಉ ಐ ಉ ಉ ಐ ಉ

Earlier that evening, Wang Jing had stood at the gate and watched Jin Xiaomei disappear through the crowd. When he retired for the night, it ended up being a sleepless night for him. He kept replaying the game with Jin Li in his head, and could not dispel the image he had of the young man and what he said about love. He remembered Jin Li's looks and considered the 'boy' strange in some way. He thought Li's face and skin too pale for a normal boy. Also, he seemed too thin for a young man, and his movements were effeminate. *Could it be that Jin Li was a girl?* This idea excited Wang Jing. He could sleep no more, and paced up and down his room. *If Jin Li were a girl... what then. Why did she come here?* He found himself simply obsessed with this idea. When sleep finally came, he had some disturbing dreams in which Jin Li had two faces. One was the face of a boy, while the other was the face of a girl. He woke up confused. *Am I attracted to this man who looks like a girl? I am already engaged.* He then thought of Dan Si, the daughter of the Prime Minister. Their families were close and the marriage had been prearranged by their parents since they were children. Dan Si was always telling her little secrets to Jing without the least reservation. However, he often forgot what she said, as he found the gossip of women boring. He knew he would rather they just remain close friends, as he saw her as more of a sister, not as his future bride. But family duty called, and he had agreed to the marriage without hesitation. His father often told him that marriage was important for a man, and it was especially important to marry a woman who would add wealth and prospects to the family. Wang Jing knew that in China's high circles, marriage had nothing to do with love.

Born into such a family as hers, Dan Si had the education and grace that was important on paper. He was aware that she tended to be overly sharp when it suited her, especially to get her own way.

Once, Dan Si had embroidered a handkerchief and gave it to him as a sign of her love. He saw it was beautifully embroidered and was touched by the girl's attentiveness. Being courteous, he said, "Thank you, I will place it against my heart." Dan Si blushed, and ran out of the room. This was the behaviour that was expected of a lady. Seeing her disappearing from his sight, Jing sighed out of frustration. He threw himself into his work.

Dan Si came to visit Wang Jing often. Wang Wengfeng could see that she was devoted to his son and treated Dan Si as his daughter-in-law, so he did not interfere. He was not sure if it was reciprocated, but Wengfeng said nothing to his son as he wanted this marriage to go ahead so that he could win the greater favour of the prime minister. *Jing is a good boy. He will do as he is told*, he thought to himself.

After stealing the first volume of *The Secret under the Mahogany tree*, Rou Rou headed towards his father's home.

Rou Rou was afraid of his father, Rou Zengnan. He was a gentleman to other people, but to his family he was overly harsh and petty. He did all he could to make their lives a misery, especially that of his daughter, as she was born by his concubine.

With *The Secret under the Mahogany tree* in his possession, he could become the best chess player in the dynasty and find the hidden treasure his father had told him about.

This evening, while Rou Zengnan was contemplating life under the star-studded sky, his servant interrupted his reverie and whispered into his master's ear that his son wished to have a word with him. *What does that useless boy want now?* he wondered. He went to the room to meet his son. "Rou Rou, what news?" he asked with a big smile on his face.

"Father, I have stolen the manual, *The Secret under the Mahogany tree*!" Rou Rou said with excitement. He held out the book for his father to see.

As soon as Rou Zengnan saw the title *The Secret under the Mahogany tree* his eyes lit up, it was the real thing! He patted his son's back, "Good boy… very good boy! Let's discover the secrets hidden in this book."

Zengnan began to turn over the pages. A poem caught his attention, "This poem seems incomplete." he said.

> *Of the chess game on the battlefield,*
> *is it a play, or a drama?*
> *If you know how to play with chess pieces,*
> *you command three armies of military might.*
> *The movement of chariots and horses*
> *traced back to the Zhou dynasty.*

"Why is there a poem in chess manual?"

Rou Zengnan wondered, and said, "I don't know… Perhaps it has something to do with the treasure code. It could be an acrostic poem. See, some of the words have been highlighted words by Wang Siyi."

"What's an acrostic poem?" Rou Rou asked.

"They are poems with an embedded code in them."

The boy moved the manual under the paraffin lamp to see it better. He read aloud the highlight words, "battlefield, war, chariots, horses, Han dynasty."

"That's it. It's a clue. This is related to an old story about Wang Siyi's treasure. Maybe the poem could tell us where the treasure is hidden. I wonder if the other part of the poem is in the other half of the manual."

A sinister smile curled a corner of Rou Zengnan mouth. "Now, son, you must acquire the second volume. We will become the top chess club in the dynasty, and we will gain the treasure. We must think of how we can bring ruin to all our other competitors."

"So be it. But how can I find the second volume?"

Rou Zengnan closed the book carefully and put it into a secret hiding place in the wall. He gazed at the place where the book was hidden, and said, "It must be in Wang Wengfeng's *Happiness Chess Club*. You shall befriend them!"

Xiaomei, woke up from the desk she had been writing on, yawned and stretched her arms. She immediately picked up where she had left off. After finishing the rewriting of the manual, she was so tired that she did not realise that it had reached noon of the next day. The bright sunshine smartened her eyes, making her a little dizzy. She rubbed them, trying to rest them. She looked around at the mess and wondered who the thief could be. *They must be a member of the chess club.* These concerns were wiped away, as if by a wand, as she remembered the heart-thrilling game with the young master of the *Happiness Chess Club*. She blushed at the thought. If her father knew about her secret he would be furious.

Troubled by these thoughts, she was at loss as to what to do next. She wondered if she should keep the theft secret from her father or tell him the truth. It was a dilemma. If she told her father about it, his hot temper was likely to turn the chess club upside down. He would search every room, and every corner of the courtyard, even overturn the bricks on the ground until he found the thief. The manual was likely to have already been taken out of the club anyway. It was a tragedy. At least, she had created a facsimile, so the knowledge could stay in the club. For good or bad, she made the decision to say nothing to her father for the time being, and investigate the case secretly herself. The thief would expose himself eventually, as fire cannot be wrapped in paper – there is no concealing the truth…

CHAPTER ELEVEN

ONE OF THE FOUR YOUNG MASTERS IN THE CAPITAL

As a past student of Wang Siyi, Rou Zengnan was an exceptional chess player. Although he was just a child when he sat at the feet of the Master, he learnt well and absorbed much. But his tuition was cut short, as we saw earlier in the story. Over the years, he continued to consolidate his skills, and now he set about to deepen his skills by studying *The Secret under the Mahogany tree*. He was excited at the prospect. As he studied the manual, Rou Zengnan found his chess strategy progressed in leaps and bounds. In just a few months, his *Talent Chess club* gained recognition amongst the better players of the city, and could even compete with the two tigers of chess — the *Plum Valley Chess Club* and *Happiness Chess Club*. A lot of young men were now joining the *Talent Chess Club* as they felt that they could learn well there. But many were equally attracted by Rou Zhengnan's showmanship. He was a man with a tongue, who could pass off lies as if they were the truth, promising these young men that if they listened to him, they would be the best chess players in the land. The courtyard swarmed with these gullible young men. He laughed with these students, promising them fame and riches if they followed him.

One of these young men asked, "Master Rou, how did you learn the strategy to win a game in only thirteen moves?"

Rou Zengnan knew this to be a stupid question, as the answer depended entirely on the skill of the opponent, but he responded with a big smile, "Be patient young man. By being indentured to our chess club you will learn... In fact, if you are good, you may learn to win in ten moves!" The would-be-student, glowed with the thought of fame such skill would bring him.

Another student asked, "Is it true that there was a manual developed by Grand Master Wang Siyi, where he wrote all his experience of the game? Some say it was lost long ago, and others say it's just a myth."

"Ha, I will kindly remind you that Chong Xu was not the only disciple of the chess master, Wang Siyi. I have already mastered all the chess strategies of that manual, including how to win in thirteen moves by sacrificing a horse. Just trust me. That's all for today, I have important government business to attend too."

The rumours spread, Rou Zengnan, was a real 'Grand Master'.

Another time, when entertaining businessmen who also played chess, whilst they were laughing and drunkenly shouting cheers, the talk naturally turned to the strategy of sacrificing a horse. One guest, who was less drunk than the rest, said purposely, "The first time I heard of this chess strategy was at a chess contest that was held in Jin Tieling's chess club. It was performed by his daughter, who is just nineteen years old.

She obviously learnt the strategy from the so-called manual, *The Secret under the Mahogany tree*."

"Oh, really? What a coincidence!" Rou Zengnan offered with sweating hands, trying hard to maintain his smile. He may be able to fool young students, but these hardened businessmen would be less easy to fool. "Yes, it's possible that there are different copies of *The Secret under the Mahogany tree*, but I can assure you my copy is the original."

"Oh. Congratulations!" His friend raised his toast and emptied his glass all at once.

Rou Zengnan could not help asking, "What does this girl look like?" He needed to know if she was going to be a threat to him. The idea that she could humiliate him horrified him. "Aha, a rare beauty! I hear all the young men of the chess club are in love with her." The other man wanted to provoke Rou Zengnan. "Apparently she is a brilliant player. Her style is unconstrained, flexible, and powerful. It seems that she is just made for chess."

Another fat faced guest cut in the conversation. "I have a portrait of her, which was painted by one of her peers who adores her."

"Do you have the portrait now?" Rou Zengnan asked with curiosity. "Yeah." The fat faced man took out a scroll from his bag. Everyone crowded around to look at this legendary chess girl. Indeed, she was very beautiful they murmured, but perhaps a bit too proud, and even haughty. Rou Zengnan surmised that with that beauty, and an iron hand in chess, she could be lethal. He returned the scroll to the fat faced man.

The first man continued, "People said that during a contest at Tieling's club she easily beat around twenty contestants, *including your son!*"

"I really wonder who has the potential to be the top chess master today?" His friend postulated.

Rou Zengnan said smugly. "Who knows. Perhaps we will find out sooner than you think."

CHAPTER TWELVE

THE PRINCE BECOMES ENAMOURED!

Jin Xiaomei's portrait had been copied and copied and spread throughout town. One day, in an upmarket tea house, Zhu Wenchun had just settled for a chat with a friend. Wenchun, a son of the prince and grandson of the emperor of the dynasty, caught a glimpse of the painting of Xiaomei that a previous customer had left on the table. Wenchun could not take his eyes off it. Noticing Wenchun staring at the painting, his friend commented, "Not only is she beautiful, but she is also known to be commanding at chess."

"Really?" said Wenchun, still entranced by the image.

"Yes. She's the daughter of Jin Tieling, the well-known chess master of the *Plum Valley Chess Club*."

The gossiper continued as if telling a story. "I have never met this girl myself, but she has a mischievous side smile that when aimed at you, can split you in two. And the moment you look into her beautiful eyes, you're forever enchanted."

Wenchun's curiosity was piqued, but as an astute young man he discounted much of what his friend said about her.

He wanted to meet this legendary girl for himself. "What's her name?"

"Jin Xiaomei."

"And you said she is a brilliant chess player. But that's impossible, women can't play chess."

"It's true. Her father was against teaching her because it is against tradition. So, she taught herself to point where he couldn't refuse her anymore. She is a girl who was endowed with both charm and a natural gift."

Wenchun marvelled at the tale. It aroused his interest, and he wanted to get to know this young woman. He asked, "Did you say that she competed with her colleagues and won all the games with them?"

"Yes, it's true. She is very good at chess, and she's also witty and intelligent."

Zhu Wenchun pondered, *a girl who can play chess must be very clever*. He rolled up the portrait determinedly and slipped it into his top. He was good at physiognomy, and so seeing Jin Xiaomei's image, he immediately realised that he had seen a treasure of a girl. He decided to find out more about her and meet her, perhaps with the goal of marrying her and making her his concubine.

∢ ∢ ∢ ∢ ∢ ∢

For several days Xiaomei was listless and spent most of her time in her room. Wen Wen was aware of this but kept quiet.

One afternoon, someone knocked on her door. Xiaomei hurried to straighten her hair and adjust the wrinkles from her clothes before opening the door. Again, it was Zhang Zheng, and again he came with a big lunch box in his hands.

"Xiaomei, it's already afternoon. Are you okay after getting up so late today?"

"No… I'm just busy." she lied.

"You looked tired. You must learn to take care of yourself. See what I brought to you today?" As he opened the box, the aroma of Gong Bao chicken filled her nostrils, she realised that she was famished.

"Thank you, brother. It's such a nice day, let's go sit by the pond." He chattered as they ate, but her mind was elsewhere. She was thinking of the young master of the rival club, Wang Jing. Then she shivered a little as she thought of the lost the manual.

"You sure you're OK Xiaomei? You seem to be so preoccupied that I'm sure you have not heard a word that I have said. What's wrong? I know you… there is something wrong. Look, you have hardly touched your food."

"It's nothing." Xiaomei tried to smile but she could not hold his gaze and looked at the pond instead.

"What did you learn today?" She asked in a lighter tone.

"Not much, we just practiced amongst ourselves." Zheng said, and then sighed, "No matter how hard we practice, we will never reach your ability."

Jin Xiaomei smiled and said, "The *Book of Changes* says anything is possible for the student who endures. So don't be despondent."

"Xiaomei, I know something is wrong," Zheng pestered.

She hated not telling him, as really, he was such a loyal friend and knew that he would always stand by her side. With that, she let out a deep sigh. Yet, she continued to say nothing.

Zheng was a wise young man and did not push it, so said, "I came to tell you something, but before I do, I want to ask you a favour. I don't know much of the chess manual, as your father never showed it to us. You and I did have a quick look one day, but it wasn't enough for me to learn from it. Anyway, I wanted to ask you if we could study it together."

Oh no, not now she thought. In a sad voice she said, "I don't have it anymore."

"Don't make fun of me. This is not a joke!"

"I don't. Did you not notice the mess in my room? It was stolen a few days ago, when I was out." Then her tears came. "When I returned, I found my room had been ransacked by someone. At first, I thought someone was looking for money, which is silly… You know how poor I am! Except for some cheap jewels, there isn't anything of value in there. Then it suddenly occurred to me to look for the manual. I had placed it at the bottom of that make-up case" she pointed at the case, which still had its contents on the floor. "I hurried to search the case, only to find that the manual was gone!"

"What?" Zheng was alarmed.

"The manual is gone." Xiaomei shrugged her shoulders, tears rolling down her cheeks.

"Does Master know?"

"I haven't seen him. I don't want to tell him about it, at least not yet. Could you keep this secret?"

"Secret? Of course." Zheng was deeply disturbed.

He was quiet, considering the options. Then, with a sudden change of direction asked, "Where were you when the manual was stolen?"

She looked at him, and a brief smile emerged. "You must promise me not to reveal this to anyone."

He laughed nervously and said, "Your secret is safe with me."

She bent over and whispered in his ear, "I not only went to the *Happiness Chess Club*... I also played a game of chess with the young chess master of the club, Wang Jing."

"What?" Zheng was worried and upset. "Aren't you afraid of Master finding out?"

Xiaomei continued with more excitement, "I was dressed as a boy. When I realised it was the son of our enemy, I vented my anger on him and goaded him into playing chess with me. He got angry and wanted to teach me a lesson in manners through chess. I wanted to squash him, so we played.

Now entranced and breathless, Zheng asked, "Who won?"

"Well... We were well-matched in the beginning, but gradually I gained the initiative. He recovered, though, and started to dominate. Towards the end it was even." She then blushed as she recalled the conversation she had with Jing before saying, "I could have won, but I suffered a major setback due to a careless move I made — he forced a stalemate."

"So, this is the first time in your adult life you did not win! Oh my. I am glad that you finally found someone who is a good match for you. But to play with the son of Wang Wengfeng, ah!"

"Yes, perhaps. But I'm annoyed with myself as I know I could have won," she said with frustration. "Obviously he is pretty good if he was able to reach a stalemate, but what does he play like?"

"He's unlike what I thought he would be. He is clever, and his game is calculating. But he is not a show-off. He... he, was nice." Her emotions were all over the place, and she let out yet another sigh.

"Did you fall in love with him?" Zheng asked dryly.

"What are you talking about? It was just a chess game!" She forced a false laugh.

"Be careful. His father and your father have unresolved resentment. There is something deeper than we know that drove them apart."

"Yes, I know. And it's strange, but Mother will not allow his name to be mentioned." She then asked, "Did you say that Mr Wang had the second volume of *The Secret under the Mahogany tree*?"

"I think so. The Master never talks about it if we ask."

"Remember the other day when I said imagine if there was a chess game where one side had the knowledge of *losing the initiative*, and we had the knowledge of *gaining the initiative*, and I wondered which strategy would end up being the most effective? Well, that's what we played. Except he did not know who I was." Waves of excitement flashed in Xiaomei's eyes again. Zheng disliked the topic and quickly finished his food.

They were quiet for a moment until she asked, "You said you had a reason for coming?"

He was clearly agitated. Petulantly he asked, "Xiaomei, if you become rich in the future, don't forget about your family, or your friends. Don't forget me."

"What do you mean?" Jin Xiaomei's eyes were big and round.

"Zhu Wenchun, the Prince, is visiting your father as we speak."

"What, why would a prince visit Father?"

"I think to propose, to ask for your hand marriage."

Xiaomei was speechless. How could she, a girl of humble circumstances attract the attention of the son of a prince! "I have not even met him!"

"God knows, he saw your portrait and fell in love with you." Zheng continued unhappily, "He is of royal blood, and has a huge fortune. Zhu Wenchun swore to his father that he won't marry any woman but you. In the beginning his father took it as a joke, but later, the young master demonstrated his determination. He said if father did not agree with him on the marriage, he would cut off his hair, go to the temple and become a monk."

"He doesn't want me just for his concubine?"

"Seems not."

"It's just a whim of a playboy. When did you hear this?"

"They are talking with your father now in the meeting room. I was in the room next door, and as you know you can hear everything from there. Come and see yourself, my dear Madam Zhu."

"Stop laughing at me!" With these words, Jin Xiaomei rushed out of the door, and ran towards the meeting room, leaving Zheng standing there alone, in low spirits.

Xiaomei wanted to rush into the study, but decided to listen in on the conversation from the other side of the door before she went in. It seemed that they had been talking for a long time. She could hear her father's voice courting the others, "My prince, I am honoured that you've shown an interest in my daughter. She would be delighted to know of Sir Zhu's interest in her. She will be happy to marry you. I must thank God for his blessing."

A different voice spoke. It was so charming and magnetic that it echoed in Xiaomei's ears. "I love your daughter very much."

Before her father could reply and the marriage affairs were settled, she burst into the room. She felt disapproving eyes staring at her, the gazes a mix of anger, curiosity, admiration, and discontent. "This is my daughter." Jin Tieling said.

Xiaomei stood there, facing the prince, her chin sightly raised. Zhu Wenchun looked at her with total adoration. Xiaomei's sudden interruption did not offend him at all. He was gallant and delighted. At that moment he knew he loved her, not only because of her beauty, but also because of her character. Xiaomei looked so different from other women he knew. She was full of life, vivacious and brave. He was convinced that this girl was unique, not only because of the portrait he saw in the tea house, but now because of this strong first impression that she'd given him. A ray of sunshine shone in from the open door, a shaft of golden light falling directly on Xiaomei, radiating a soft and graceful light. She could not have been presented in a more alluring way. Zhu Wenchun was unable to move his gaze.

"Daughter, kowtow in the presence of royalty," Tieling said with fury. "You are to respect Prince Zhu, his son Prince Wenchun, and the official aid to Prince Zhu, Tong Fong."

She briefly kowtowed to each in turn. When she straightened Xiaomei shot a glance at these people who were arranging her marriage without her knowledge or consent. She glared at her father. Xiaomei summoned her courage, and asked with her subtle side smile, "Father, are you talking about me with these men?"

Zhu Wenchun took the opportunity to further appraise Jin Xiaomei. This is a proud girl, she really is more vivacious and lovely than her portrait. Her eyes, which were appraising him, shone with intelligence. They seemed to penetrate his soul. Though the prince was full of admiration for Jin Xiaomei, his father Prince Zhu held a different opinion, as he saw something uncontrollable about this girl and her arrogance. The father was almost sure that this girl was not the child-bearing type, and he decided that he did not want her to be his daughter-in-law. *If my son must have this girl, she must be his concubine, not his first wife!*

"Let's me introduce my daughter to you." Jin Tieling said with some embarrassment. "This is Jin Xiaomei, my only daughter. Xiaomei, this is Prince Zhu. And this is Prince Zhu Wenchun, the son of the prince." Then Jin Tieling turned towards Master Zhu and said flatteringly, "Though she may have forgotten her manners, she can be quite a lady when she tries. I am sure that Xiaomei will be a good wife. I feel so ashamed that she was so indulged by me. I believe she will find her rightful place."

The old prince Zhu nodded his head, dissatisfied with this young lady's behaviour. There are a thousand beauties in the imperial city with higher birth and better manners. He could not understand what his son saw in this Jin Xiaomei – and she plays chess!

Xiaomei could feel the sharp and critical eyes of the old prince. She blushed unconsciously, and then even more so when she became aware of the of the young prince staring at her. If he could rudely stare at her then she would do the same to him. She turned to face him and slightly nodded her head to him. Xiaomei pondered to herself, *Zhu Wenchun has the reputation of being one of the four young masters in the capital. However, I would never marry him, as by doing so I am likely to sacrifice my chess career. He is likely to want me to bear a lot of children and be a good mother.* She said firmly, "I will never willingly marry anyone who I do not love. Not even a prince."

"Ha-ha" Zhu Wenchun clapped his hands, "Not only is she beautiful, but she is also independent. A rare beauty, a rare beauty!"

Jin Xiaomei gave him a look, greatly disturbed; alas, how unfair fate is! She was resolute. Jin Tieling was burning with anger and scolded her harshly. He had lost face in front of royalty, and his glare at her expressed just that. "How could you say that? It is not up to you to decide your own marriage affairs!"

Jin Xiaomei knew she was likely to add wood to the fire, but she was unable to stop herself. She turned to Zhu Wenchun and asked, "You don't know me, so how can you love me, and how can you expect me to love you when this is the first time I have meet you?"

Zhu Wenchun was speechless. She had just shred traditional feminine values to pieces and disobeyed her father. He smiled to himself and after a few minutes of struggling with his uncertainty, he was more determined than before. He would marry Jin Xiaomei at all costs, even if it meant giving up the title of the prince. Zhu Wenchun closed his fan, stood up, and with assured dignity said, "I can promise that I will love you for who you are. I would not want to make a fish fly like a bird."

The answer was so unexpected to her that her suspicions stirred again. *There are too many dandies and good liars in this world! How could I, a person of low blood, attract the attention of a royal blood?* To her, it could be the biggest joke, or her biggest tragedy. *He probably has romantic relations with other ladies, and now wants a different flavour.* Xiaomei knew who she was, and she never dreamed a sparrow would become a swan. She regarded his profession of love as just his moment of fantasy. Jin Xiaomei smiled with dignity, though she was a little uneasy in her mind, and replied, "Thank you, but I still doubt whether marrying you would be wise. I am afraid you will regret your decision someday. Even if you considered the marriage with me to be romantic at this moment, as time passes, you will soon get tired of me. We would then both hate each other. Please forget about me before it is too late."

With these words, Xiaomei gave a quick bow and left the room, paying no attention to her father who was sitting there, totally stunned.

CHAPTER THIRTEEN
THE SECOND GAME

Xiaomei hurried back to her room, trembling all over, not only out of anger, but also out of fear. She had refused a prince of royal blood. What would this bring upon her and her family? They could be put in prison for her insolence.

Her thoughts started meandering. The game with Wang Jing suddenly came to mind and she knew she was infatuated with him. If she had to marry someone, she wanted to marry a man like Wang Jing, with whom she could talk the whole night until dawn. Even on a cold winter night, they would sit and play chess together by the fire until they got tired. She could read Wang Jing's mind, and he would read hers. This was the kind of life she thought she wanted! *What will be will be*, she thought. She looked at herself in the mirror and touched her chin with her hands. How thin and sharp she looked! Her father made it difficult for her to meet other people outside the club, but she was unwilling to give in. She would meet Wang Jing again, tomorrow!

❦ ❧ ❦ ❦ ❧ ❦

As before, Xiaomei passed through the splendid corridor and entered *The Happiness Chess Club*. There were many guests in the club, like rabbits in a warren. She lifted the curtain hanging on the door to enter the parlour, only to see a beautiful lady leaning on Wang Jing's arm. Xiaomei immediately turned pale. She hurried to drop the curtain, feeling her heart thump as if were about to burst from her chest. She leaned heavily on a table nearby, trying not to show her weakness and troubled thoughts. Wang Jing had noticed her and immediately came out, accompanied by the lady. He touched her sleeves and said enthusiastically, "Jin Li, how long you have kept me waiting! You are here at last! The chess table in my room is always waiting for you. But... but are you okay? You do not look well." Then Wang Jing hastened to introduce the lady at his side, "This is my fiancée, Dan Si. We grew up together. Dan Si, this is my chess friend Jin Li. His chess skills equal mine."

Dan Si and Jin Xiaomei politely smiled at each other. Guided by her womanly instinct, Dan Si immediately knew that Jin Xiaomei was a girl disguised as a boy. Xiaomei felt Dan Si's eyes penetrate her disguise and lowered her head, fearing that her pretence would be uncovered. But after a sly smile and slight sideways glance, Dan Si kept resolutely silent.

Xiaomei was led by Wang Jing to the chess-table. She was absent-minded as the advent of Dan Si had crushed her confidence. Not only was she sure Dan Si knew Xiaomei was a girl, but she was betrothed to Jing; *what a fool I was to think that such a handsome and eligible man such as Jing would not already have someone on his arm.* Dazed, she fought to compose herself. Wang Jing took her hands and lead her to her seat. He felt Jin Li's hands were as soft, like those of a young girl. The silky touch of those hands gave Wang Jing an electric shock. His heart could not stop thumping. His male instinct somehow made him reluctant to free Xiaomei's hands. He wore a roughish smile on his face, and asked, "Why are you so impolite to me? You were about to leave without saying anything. I thought we were friends?"

Jin Xiaomei blushed at this genuine intimacy and lowered her head, trying to avoid revealing her secret. "I'm sorry, but I am preoccupied with something. It is not your fault. In fact, I may not be such a good opponent today."

"May I ask you what the trouble is?"

"I would rather keep it to myself, thank you."

Wang Jing was excited. This did not make sense to him. Starting the game, he was the first to move. This time, he used his pawn as an opening, an opening known as the Angel's Guide. He wanted to see Xiaomei's next movement, to uncover her true nature. *Is he actually a girl? Why are his hands so soft and smooth?*

Jin Xiaomei guessed what Wang Jing was thinking, so she did not move the cannon to attack the pawn, which was the opening he was expecting. She also chose the pawn opening. This bewildered Wang Jing.

Xiaomei was too distracted to play. What did Wang Jing say about his fiancée? *They grew up together and played together! How could I break up this happy couple?* Xiaomei sighed. How unfair fate is! *The worst thing in one's life is to fall in love with someone at the wrong time.* She could not help comparing herself to Dan Si. She knew the family name. Everyone knew she was the Prime Minister's daughter. *She is in a different class.* Xiaomei's eyelashes moistened. She even started wondering whether it would be a good idea to just marry the young prince and bear a dozen silly children for him!

So consumed with these thoughts, she did not notice that Wang Jing's chariot had already crossed the river, and his troops were marching towards Xiaomei's palace. She had been making moves without even noticing what she was doing.

Now alarmed, she had to recover her composure quickly and return to reality. She felt tremendous pressure to turn the situation around. Pearls of sweat appeared on her forehead. Wang Jing noticed his guest's unusual behaviour. He looked absent-minded and ill. Something was wrong. He asked, "Li are you unwell?"

"Well, umm… What makes you say so?"

"If you feel unwell, let's play chess another time."

"I am fine, thank you." She said with determination. She took a deep breath and tried to concentrate on the chessboard, remembering her father's words, "Never give up. Fight until the last piece is gone." Before the game was over, she would have ample opportunity to turn this situation around. She clenched her jaw and moved a horse.

Wang Jing attacked with aggression. She did not even notice that her other horse was attacked by his cannon. "Ah." Xiaomei cried out and turned pale. Wang Jing took advantage of the situation to dominate by advancing rapidly, and checking her king with two cannons, one on the top of the palace, the other one at the bottom. Xiaomei always considered it the most devious chess strategy, which she abhorred as it made her feel that she had no way to escape her fate.

"What's the matter?" Wang Jing was surprised to see Jin Xiaomei so pale.

"Why did you use this strategy to check my king!" Xiaomei jumped to her feet and complained unreasonably, "I hate this strategy. I warn you… if you want me to play chess with you again in the future, you should never employ this strategy to check my king!" Xiaomei blurted out this nonsense, and regretted it immediately as soon as the words were spoken. She could not help blushing.

Wang Jing was totally at a loss as what to say. "You are not well!" Wang Jing spoke with concern. "Can I order you some water or tea?"

Xiaomei regretted her rudeness. She hurried to apologise and said, "No. I am so sorry. I was terrible. I am embarrassed."

"As you are feeling so unwell, let's forget this game. We can play another time?"

"Yes, you are right. I am sorry for my rudeness. I will return and be better mannered, and play better."

"Very well."

Xiaomei got up from her seat, intending to leave, but she could not resist the temptation to look back and cast a furtive glance at the lady who reappeared at Wang Jing's side. Their eyes met again. Xiaomei quickly lowered her head and left with Dan Si was still watching her. Xiaomei was almost sure Dan Si knew her secret.

CHAPTER FOURTEEN
HUGE WAVES IN JIANG HU

Now they were able to use the strategies of *The Secret under the Mahogany tree,* the *Talent Chess Club* had become well-known. Rou Zengnan was the self-proclaimed successor of Wang Siyi.

Jia Wuhu from *Peace Life Chess Club* visited his old friend Rou Zengnan. After they indulged in much drinking, Jia Wuhu asked, "Rou, have you heard any news about the secret treasure that was hidden by Wang Siyi? When you were a disciple of Wang Siyi, did he ever mention it? Apparently, the code for its hiding place is in a manual called *The Secret under the Mahogany tree.* Now that you are his successor, are you the custodian of the treasure? People say you have the chess manual. Brother Rou, do you know where the treasure is hidden?"

Rou Zengnan smiled awkwardly, "I don't know where it is. If I knew, I would have been a rich man by now."

"I guess so Brother Rou, but your secret is already well known in Jiang Hu. I hope you don't mind if I tell you frankly that every chess club is looking for clues to find the treasure.

Every person who has recently visited you could be a spy. Your secret chess manual is no longer safe in your hands. It might be stolen one day." Jia Wuhu tried to convince Rou Zengnan.

On hearing what his friend had to say, Rou Zengnan gave him a withering glare, before quickly recollecting himself and bursting out with hoarse laughter. "I will be vigilant. Wait here."

Rou Zengnan rose and went into another room. He pressed a hidden button next to his chair, whereby a secret door opened leading to a small clandestine room. It contained a cupboard with a golden box inside. Rou Zengnan entered and carefully opened the golden box. Then with caution, he took out the classical manual. Returning to his guest, he said, "This is what Wang Siyi passed on to me." Rou Zengnan held the manual in his hands and gave it to Jia Wuhu to have a look. Rou Zengnan wore a large smile, a perfect mask that hid his true thoughts. He stared at the manual with bulging eyes. Never in his lifetime would he imagine that he'd have the chance to look at this secret and sacred book!

"Can I open it and look inside?" Jia Wuhu tried to conceal his excitement.

"Well, just a quick look. It was given to me by the Master with the instruction to retain its secrets," Rou Zengnan said generously.

As usual, when opened, the poem on the front page was seen. Jia considered it strange that there was only a part of a poem, but he dismissed the thought and quickly turned over one page after another to see the chess moves and strategies. He was greatly absorbed until Rou Zengnan rudely snatched the book from his hands. With a chuckle he said, "Don't forget that you were not given the privilege of reading this book by the master."

Jia Wuhu, as a devoted chess player, felt a flash of resentment. He quickly recovered himself. He felt like a starving fox that about to eat its kill, only to have it seized by a larger animal. Jia Wuhu carefully hid his greed and gave a chuckle to cover his annoyance, "Forgive me, I was so absorbed I forgot my manners. The book is indeed a rare treasure."

"Oh no harm done." Rou Zengnan smiled and returned to the other room where he replaced the manual inside the golden box. But Jia Wuhu shuffled so that he could see into the other room, where he stared at the golden box with avarice. He had already started plotting to gain possession of the manual. He must have it.

Zengnan noticed his friend had changed position as he came back into the room.

Jia Wuhu said, "Zengnan, how old is your daughter this year?"

"My daughter?" Rou Zengnan said carelessly, "This year she will be fifteen."

"Fifteen, she is coming of age. My youngest son is twenty years. He is not married because he devotes himself to study. If you do not frown down on us, I humbly request my son marry your daughter."

Rou Zengnan was secretly delighted to hear this, as he needed allies desperately. Still, he acted as if he had to give it a second thought to gain more bargaining power.

"Don't you think it is a desirable match for our families?" Jia pressed.

"Hmmm, perhaps."

"I will give you 500 silver taels."

"Ummm, errr... She had made mention that she likes the eldest boy from the Dong family. They are well connected and a good family, and have lots of wealth from his father's metal business."

"Brother Rou, if we become one family, we could merge our chess clubs into one... We would be the biggest in the dynasty. And... with 1000 silver taels, it's a good deal right?"

Rou Zengnan acted as if he was suddenly enlightened. He said finally, "Yes, you could be right. My daughter and your son will make a fine match."

≪ ≫ ≪ ≪ ≫ ≪

Rou Feifei heard the news that her father agreed for her to marry the son of Jia Wuhu. Upon hearing the news, she dissolved into tears. She had never met this young man before, what if he was ugly and wicked? As much as she wanted to tell her father that she is not an object to be traded, she dared not, as she was scared at the prospect of another thrashing. Rou Zengnan despised his daughter, especially when she stared at him with those penetrating eyes of hers, half-submissive, half-rebellious. He was glad to get rid of her. Rou Zengnan said, "Well, aren't you grateful? You should be grateful that I found a man worthy of you. I can tell you, against tradition, I had to pay the father to take you into his family. I did this for your sake."

Rou Feifei was grief-stricken. She looked at her father in despair and cried, "I would rather never have been born!"

"You ungrateful thing! What's the use of being a woman? Nothing, but to give birth to children, and to enlarge family connections. Remember, my ungrateful daughter, it is I who gave life to you."

As Xiaomei, now twenty years of age, was now regarded as a master chess player, Jin Tieling submitted to her advice. She persuaded Jin Tieling to teach his students the best strategies from the manual instead of hiding everything from them. Tieling was not happy when his guests told him that other chess clubs were teaching the same chess strategy that Jin Xiaomei had learnt. "Xiaomei, is there something that you have kept from me?" Jin Tieling had a long face, as he knew only his chess club knew the strategy of the first volume. But now, apparently, all of Jiang Hu knew it and applied it. Someone must have leaked the information from the *Plum Valley Chess Club*.

Xiaomei looked at her father, ashamed, but said nothing.

"Is there something that you are hiding from me?" he asked again.

She thought that Father was referring to her secret visits to the *Happiness Chess Club*.

"No, nothing." she lied and blushed.

"But these secrets can only come from the *Secret under the Mahogany tree* that I entrusted to you. The *Talent Chess Club* has recently become extremely popular and has started attracting a huge number of students and guests. We are getting fewer and fewer people coming to our club. I'm not joking. More birds flutter at our doors in the morning than regular patrons. Have you any idea how this could have happened?" Jin Tieling persisted.

Xiaomei, embarrassed, did not know how to tell her father that the book was missing. Now, knowing that the survival of the *Plum Valley Chess Club* was at stake, she frowned and said, "I am sorry Father... I should have told you. A thief entered my room and stole the manual. I was so sad and hoped to get it back, somehow."

"Stolen! You mean we no longer have it?"

Xiaomei narrated the event with despair, "But Father, I knew the book so well I made a copy." "Oh" is all he said, as he half collapsed onto a chair, covering his face with his hands. Xiaomei was anguished by his despair. She started to say something, but he waved her to be quiet. Xiaomei sighed with relief because she was afraid of his fierce temper. But her father was calm, seemingly thinking. At last, he spoke, "It seems that the thief came from our own ranks. So how long has the thief been hiding in our club? If all he wanted was to learn the strategy of the secret manual, he shouldn't have been worried as one day I would have taught him. There must be a more compelling reason for stealing the book."

"If I remember correctly there were some highlighted characters in the poem including battlefield, war, chariots, and horses, and Han dynasty." Tieling nodded his head in remembrance. It was so strange that these characters were highlighted. Was there a secret behind that?

"Father, what is lost is lost, there is no point in fretting. We need to develop a strategy, to strike back."

"Yes but how?"

"When you want to end a game of a weaker opponent you set your pieces to stalk their king," she said, "If we try to catch their king directly, the opponent will be on guard. If we try to catch the thief directly, he and his accomplice will also be on their guard. We will allow the enemies to expose themselves. We will also teach our students the strategies from the secret manual. That way it will reduce their power."

Tieling looked old, but when he nodded agreement there was fire in his eyes. He had also been thinking. "I do not think it could be Wang Wengfeng's club that stole our manual. If they did, they would have combined it with their manual and would have become the supreme club in the land. And, as *The Talented Chess Club* seems to have flourished of late, all clues point to them. Anyway, whoever stole the manual is likely to try and steel Wengfeng's manual. We must watch and listen vary carefully."

With a deep breath of anticipation, she started, "Father. There is a way to find out if the *Happiness Chess club* stole our manual..." She went on to tell of the two times she had been to the club dressed as a man and played against Wang Jing. Tieling was alarmed and became agitated, but said nothing, allowing her to continue. He became excited at the thought of the stalemate. She made no mention of her infatuation with Jing. "So, Father, I will dress as a man again to play 'my friend Jing'. After our stalemate, he will be more determine to show he is the best player. If they stole the manual and studied it, which they surely would have, it will be difficult for him to not incorporate the strategies from the first part of the manual in his game. It would have become a part of his game. Father, I think I am a clever enough player to detect if methods from the first half of the manual are included. That way we will know if we should focus our efforts on the *Happiness Chess club* or the *Talent Chess* club."

Tieling did not like the idea, but could see the merit in it. He reluctantly agreed.

❧ ❧ ❧ ❧ ❧ ❧

Several months passed. Tieling now respected Xiaomei's ability so much that he allowed her to help run the club. With her help, the *Plum Valley Chess Club's* business began to grow again. Students and guests were attracted by the combination of the 'Old Master' and his beautiful and masterly chess playing daughter. This worried Rou Zengnan, who secretly passed on a message to his son, "Get the second volume of the book, now!"

From early childhood, Rou Rou thought the world a crazy and hostile place. His younger sister Rou Feifei was his only friend and comfort. She was always there for him, willing to hear his complaints and wipe the tears off his face, which were many as a child in that household.

Rou Feifei longed to live an ordinary life. She felt herself a prisoner of the family. The news of her upcoming marriage pained her and added to the sorrows of her wounded heart. After a brief exchange of dowry and other prearranged formalities, Rou Feifei was married to Jia Tianjing, Jia Wuhu's son. Jia Tianjing was equally reluctant. He greatly protested to his father, as he had already fallen in love with another woman. This woman was no other but Dan Si. Once, he went to the temple, lit incense sticks, and asked for a blessing. There he encountered Dan Si, dressed in a white gown, also lighting incense. The wind was blowing softly, and her long black hair was flowing in the wind. Wang Tianjing stood there, watching Dan Si who passed by, completely absorbed by her beauty. He reached out a hand, trying to clutch Dan Si's long dress, but she had already passed as if just a vision.

"Father, you use me as a pawn in one of your chess games!" But there was to be no miracle for Wang Tianjing. His father arranged the marriage, and that was that. To soften the blow, Jia Wuhu said to his son, "Once we get our hands on the treasure, you can do whatever you please. You could get a dozen concubines. I just want that treasure!" Wang Tianjing finally agreed.

Jia Wuhu's family's courtyard was decorated with strange stones, mirroring the sharpness and roughness of the Jia family. The moment Jia Tianjing uncovered his bride's veil, he found a pale-faced girl, sobbing so hard that her eyes were red and spongy. When alone, Jia Tianjing snarled, "Do you think you are the only victim of this marriage transaction? If it were not for your father and the secret chess manual, I would rather let my father cut me to pieces than marry you. Can't you stop crying? Tonight, after I have used you, you will go to your own bed."

Rou Feifei swallowed the tears and lowered her chin. She collapsed with anguish. For her, this wedding was also her funeral. Then in a moment of retaliation, with flame in her eyes, she said, "You may use me for sex. I will not resist. But you will never get satisfaction from me."

As he has seen his father do often enough, he slapped her face. She did not flinch and continued glaring at him.

And so, their marriage started. Once she heard Jia Tianjing talking about the manual, she remembered a conversation between her father and her brother and a desperate idea occurred to her. She wanted to perform one last rebellious act against her father; *with no hope of life, it is my end. Goodbye, beautiful, sweet blue sky. Goodbye, my dear and caring brother! And goodbye my sweet childhood dreams.*

Rou Feifei laughed a dry laugh and taunted him, "I know where the book is. But I will never tell you. You can rot in poverty for all I care."

"Where is the manual? Where?" Jia Tianjing asked desperately.

"I will never tell you where it is."

Grabbing her throat he shouted in her face, "Tell me!"

"Go on, do it. Strangle me and put me out of my misery. The secret of that book will die with me."

Knowing it was pointless to kill her, he roughly pushed her away and left the room.

Rou Feifei knew what she was going to do. After, when she was gone, they would fight and kill each other for that damned manual and supposed treasure. It would be her final act, to destroy all the people she hated. She would be sorry about her brother Rou Rou, but he was just as greedy as the rest.

"I will tell you where the book is." she said to her husband when he next entered the room.

"Why would you tell me now? Is it because you want a share of the treasure?"

"I have my own reasons… The book is in a golden box in my father's secret room. If you enter the study, you will find a chair in the middle of the room. There is a hidden button in the chair. Press the button, and the wall behind the bookshelf will open. If you go inside, you will find a small golden box. The manual is inside."

"How do you know all this?"

"I overheard a conversation between my father and my brother." And with that, the new bride cursed the man secretly in her heart, begging God to mete out justice.

Jia Tianjing hurried to his father. Seeing his son outside the bridal room, the father was surprised. "Why are you not with your bride?"

"Father, I am so good in bed, she told me where Rou Zengnan hides the manual."

The father was proud of his son's sexual prowess, *just like me* he thought. But he was more concerned with the manual and said, "Where is it?"

He quickly told him.

"We must take action, now." Said Jia Wuhu, "Before he changes the hiding place again." "Yes, of course."

Father and son headed to Rou Zengnan's house, their hearts racing, both determined that glory and wealth were at hand.

The night was pitch black and cold, perfect for their mission. As they walked, they were silent, and kept to the shadows. Upon arriving at the villa, they crawled low against the wall.

Jia Wuhu was surprised that there was no guards or servants at the gate. The house looked bleak in the dark. He exchanged a look with his son. Jia Tianjing whispered, "Maybe it was because everyone in the family was drunk, and they're now sleeping it off." This after all was the wedding day of Rou Feifei and Jia Tianjing.

They tip-toed through an open gate and entered the courtyard. Jia Wuhu's sight was sharp, even in the dark. The treasure hunters' hearts beat furiously. Quietly, they tried some of the doors leading onto the courtyard and found one that was not barred. Father and son crept inside. All was quiet. As their eyes adjusted to the extra darkness, they eventually found the study. In the dim light they saw the chair, and fumbled around it until they located the button. After one press, the wall behind the bookshelf opened. They grinned to each other and went inside. In there it was much darker, but eventually they found the golden box. Both rushed to open the box, but the son stopped half-way, and with respect said, "Father, please."

The father quickly opened the box without the least bit of suspicion as to why the box was unlocked. There was a book inside, but it was too dark to read the title. He opened the book to try and go through the pages to confirm if it was the manual.

Suddenly, Jia Wuhu yelled in agitation. His fingers became numb, and he clutched his throat, as if he were being strangled. Jia Wuhu dropped to the floor and rolled around in the last throws of life. Jia Tianjing stood frozen in the dark, not knowing what was happening. Then he heard the strangled hiss of his father's last words, "Avenge me. Do you hear... find the treasure. The Rou family ... are enemies, forever... kill them!" As the voice stopped, so did the movement on the floor. Jia Tianjing ran out of the room, the house, and out of the property in panic. He did not stop running until he reached his house.

The next morning, Rou Zengnan arose with a slight hangover. He told his servant to hurry with his breakfast, when a messenger entered and whispered something to him. Rou Zengnan nodded his head, and asked, "Dead! Both of them?"

The servant said timidly "No, the father is dead. The son escaped."

Hearing this, Rou Zengnan was so furious that he kicked the wooden chair in front of him, narrowly missing the messenger. He shouted "Get out! You lame duck. Find out where that stupid piglet Jia Tianjing is." The messenger nodded his head, kowtowed, and hurried away, his hands trembling.

Rou Zengnan was frustrated, and felt a severe headache coming. It was shameful to allow the fish to slip through a well-weaved net. His secret about the treasure would never be safe again. Sooner or later, everyone in Jiang Hu would start looking for the treasure. Fear crept into his heart. He was racing against time to find out where the treasure was hidden. Rou Zengnan needed to push his son to realise his goal.

Now that the *Plum Valley Chess Club* was expanding and flourishing, it was immersed in a happy atmosphere. Little did they know that this was the calm before the storm. Though Xiaomei knew there was a spy in the club, she still could not figure out who he was. She was sure sooner or later the thief would expose himself.

Wang Wengfeng was worried that his competitor, the *Plum Valley Chess Club*, kept growing in scale. This angered Wang Wengfeng, for there were few things that he liked less than being beaten by Jin Tieling. All the old grudges overwhelmed him, making him restless and ruthless. He could not bear hearing the family name 'Jin' when mentioned by others. The name was like a mirror, reflecting his wickedness and cowardliness. It painfully reminded him that he scorned the love that claimed his heart. Jin Tieling was always an upright person, and was capable of loyalty and honesty, which Wang Wengfeng admired but could never emulate. He felt overshadowed by Jin Tieling and made a pledge to ruin his former friend. His hatred was accumulating day by day, as if excreted toxins were poisoning his life, making him bitter. It was Wang Wengfeng himself who gave the start-up money to Jin Tieling for his chess club, so he believed that he also had the right to destroy it by own hands.

From time to time, Wang Wengfeng could not help recalling the memories of those carefree days in Plum Valley when they both studied the game under Chong Xu. In those days, he and Jin Tieling were like brothers, inseparable, following each other like shadows. But the truth was that he hated himself more than Jin Tieling. For all those years, his own conscience tortured him. Yes, he had married a high society lady, but his life was empty. He still loved Wen Wen. Wang Wengfeng knew that he must find an opportunity to ruin Jin Tieling.

About that time, Dan Si seemed to become more and more important in Wang Wengfeng's eyes. Having secured the engagement to his son since their childhood, Wang Wengfeng was afraid that his careless son would do something to break up with this innocent but well-connected girl. Wang Wengfeng decided to visit Dan Si's father in order to settle the marriage date as soon as possible.

Dan Si's father, Dan Shiran, welcomed Wang Wengfeng with a warm hug and great hospitality. He invited Wang Wengfeng into his study. They had a pleasant talk with a cup of wine. They spoke about current politics, the latest gossip, and the most topical issues of the return of explorer Zheng He from his sea voyage of the distant east. He had been received by the emperor only yesterday.

"What do you think of Admiral Zheng's voyage? Did he really go that far?" Wang Wengfeng asked curiously.

"His ship's journals reflect he travelled across a vast ocean. This was confirmed by the journals of the other officers. He also bought back fruits, and items that we have never seen. He encountered different races of people and survived many adventures on the way. The voyage took two years."

"What inspired him the most?"

"He discovered a vast land far to the east of us. It is populated with black natives, who are friendly to trade. Some of the journals have sketches of these people — they look very different to us. They returned with seeds for some crops, which we are interested in sowing. Zheng wants to refit his ship and go back, but the emperor has other ideas and has forbidden him to do so."

"It must have been an amazing trip. Zheng He has seen a great deal of the world." Wang Wengfeng sipped his wine, and continued, "Why did the emperor cancel his further explorations? It's a real pity, the timing of the exploration is perfect. The best time for our national prosperity."

"Yes, a pity. It was because of the troubles from pirates on our coastline. Some pirates called themselves Dutch, who speak bad Chinese, while some are Japanese. They claimed to come to trade with us, but they caused a lot of trouble near our border. The emperor decided he needed Zheng He to remain to help close the door and restore peace."

When Dan Shiran ended the topic, Wang Wengfeng got down to business. "Brother Dan, I nearly forgot why I came. I want to discuss the marriage between Dan Si and my son. To set the date?"

"Oh. Yes, of course." Dan Shiran smoothed his beard and smiled with a double meaning, "Well, it seems that Dan Si's not so happy. She complains that your son ignores her much of the time."

"Oh, I'm sure that has no meaning. He has been working very hard." but Wang Wengfeng was annoyed and he secretly cursed his son's inattention. *He could spoil the entire 'deal'. How could he be so thoughtless and dare to neglect the daughter of the prime minister!* But he continued, "Well, to the point, it is always a pleasant thing for parents to see their children get married as soon as possible. As we are old friends it will surely be a happy union. My son asked me to come and propose the marriage date."

"Ha-ha." Dan Shiran smiled, "Being old as we are, what else do we want from life? Nothing but the happiness of our children."

"You are right. Which date do you think is appropriate?"

The two fathers began to turn over the almanac and calculate the best day according to Wang Jing and Dan Si's dates of birth. The two fathers agreed upon the month of November.

"Everything is settled. I'm delighted." Wang Wengfeng clapped his hands and laughed.

"Yes. It will be a fine wedding."

They lapsed into silence for a moment, until Wengfeng spoke. "Brother Dan, I have one thing to request from you."

"What is it?"

"Have you ever heard of the *Plum Valley Chess Club*?"

"Yes, I have. Your club and *Plum Valley Chess Club* are like two dragons fighting for a pearl." "It is good to have competition... But Jin Tieling now teaches his disciples the strategy described in the book *The Secret under the Mahogany tree* that was passed to me by our Master Chong Xu to save for prosperity. There are two volumes of the book, one titled *How to gain the initiative*, and the other *How to lose the initiative*. When I was washing one day, Jin Tieling stole the first volume. This was against Master Chong Xu wishes, and that's why our friendship ended... Jin Tieling is a thief. Anyway, I did not want to cause a fuss, and so I left it to him. But now this has provoked turmoil in Jiang Hu. Crowds of people go to his chess club just to catch a glimpse of this legendary strategy, which was said to be lost long ago."

"A secret book? What kind of secret book?"

"It's called *The Secret under the Mahogany tree.*"

"Did Chong Xu tell you anything more about that book? Why does it bear the title *The Secret under the Mahogany tree?* What kind of secret does it hold?"

"I don't know. Quite to my shame, our Master said nothing about it."

Dan Shiran asked whilst stroking his beard "Do you want to get the first volume of the book back?"

"Of course. It was Master's wish that I keep the book safe from exploitation. I think the entire club should be shut down because it is so corrupt. It is a disgrace to our wonderful game."

"Ha-ha. That's easy enough." Dan Shiran said, "You provide the evidence, and I will supply the civil case to bury him and his club."

"Thank you, my brother."

"But now I have one request of you my Dear Wengfeng. As a father, I humbly ask you tell Wang Jing to spend more time with Dan Si. I have seen her whimpering in her room many times. And, I don't know if you know, but there seems there may be another that has captured his heart."

☙ ❧ ☙ ☙ ❧ ☙

As he left the Prime Minister's office, he beamed an evil smile. Dan Shiran and Wang Wengfeng had discussed that they needed to find an insider among Jin Tieling's disciples, who would be willing to betray him. In fact, as if by miracle, he quickly found such a person. And more precisely, the young man came to him. This person was Rou Rou, the son of Rou Zengnan. Rou Rou burst into tears in front of Wang Wengfeng to complain about his chess master, purporting that Jin Tieling was bad to his disciples.

Overcome with joy, Wang Wengfeng did not even have the slightest suspicion that Rou Rou might have his own reasons to infiltrate his chess club. Rou Rou played his usual role of the rejected boy. Wang Wengfeng was deeply touched by Rou Rou's tears and misfortunes, believing what he said without a second thought. That was why Rou Rou sought refuge in his chess club. It was well known that Jin Tieling had bouts of temper. It made sense that Jin Tieling was hiding something. Wang Wengfeng also kept the secret book himself, and only showed it to his son. Wang Wengfeng was not on his guard, beguiled by this miserable young man. However, as always, whatever the reason was, a traitor could never be trusted. In Wang Wengfeng's opinion, Rou Rou was just a pawn in his game of deception.

Rou Rou face was a picture misery as he explained his story, "I became one of the disciples of Jin Tieling. Of course, we went to the *Plum Valley Chess Club* attracted by Jin Tieling's famous reputation. However, Jin Tieling was not a chess master at all, but a person full of vanity. I was not treated like a disciple, more like a servant, having to do all the hard work in the club and run errands for him. All I have learned is Jin Tieling's meanness and pettiness. He treats his disciples with hostility, and often scolds us because of tiny mistakes. He is a lazy teacher. For almost three years I have learned nothing but how to open the game. He only looks with a friendly eye on his first disciple, Zhang Zheng, maybe because this upstart is in cahoots with his daughter." Rou Rou frowned in frustration.

"Yes. He has a daughter, I believe," Wang Wengfeng could not help feeling moved.

"She is as bad as he is."

"What does his daughter look like?" Wang Wengfeng was thinking of Wen Wen's beauty and wondered whether she resembled her mother.

"His daughter…" Rou Rou felt embarrassed. He did not know how to answer this question. Rou Rou's mind ran fast. Why does Wang Wengfeng care so much about Jin Tieling's daughter? "She is quite common." Rou Rou felt himself sweating. He was trying to think of a good answer, "She is beautiful, but it is only skin deep."

Wang Wengfeng was satisfied to have found the right person, a typical traitor and a good liar. Though he did not trust Rou Rou, treacherous as the boy was, at least he would not miss this opportunity.

"So what do you want to do."

"I humbly ask if I can join your club."

"But you already have a master. You know the custom. Once a master, always a master, as he is also a father-like figure, too."

"He has never been a real master to me."

"Fine. Rou, from now on you will be a member of The *Happiness Chess Club*… Congratulations! We will teach you the beautiful game of chess. But… but if you want me to help you get even with Jin Tieling you must continue pretending you are still a member of his club. You must continue going there to collect evidence of his neglecting his disciples and being untrue to the chess ethos."

"Yes Master. I will do so."

To be honest, Rou Rou was disgusted with himself, as he knew he had been treated with kindness by Jin Tieling and his family. Was he not selling his soul for the sake of money? Yes, for the treasure.

"All right young man. What do you want from me in return?" Wang Wengfeng smiled brightly and asked.

"Nothing. I just want to learn to play chess. I want to become a champion."

And with that lie, Rou Rou kowtowed three times before leaving.

❧ ❧ ❧ ❧ ❧ ❧

That evening, after the meeting with Wang Wengfeng, Rou Rou went to his father, who had been waiting for him. "Any news?" he asked impatiently.

"Wang Wengfeng has agreed to accept me as his student." Rou Rou said with an expressionless face. "Good!" he said, patting his son's shoulder as if patting a cat, "Wait for the chance to get the second volume of the book. You and I will become rich."

"Father, Wang Wengfeng asked me to spy for him at the *Plum Valley Chess Club*."

"Really? There comes our opportunity. You must win Wang Wengfeng's confidence since he uses you as a pawn. When two dogs fight for a bone, a third runs away with it."

Rou Rou was still expressionless, refusing to show the emotions that stirred within. He asked, "Do other chess clubs know about the secret book?"

"Probably." His father grumbled.

"How come?" Rou Rou's eyes were as sharp as an eagle's, as he remembered that the other person who knew this secret was his sister. If people in Jiang Hu all knew about the secret book, the source must be his sister. It meant that his sister's life was in danger.

"Do you care?" His father interrogated him with the pretence of carelessness.

"No, not a bit."

Rou Rou did not go back to Jin Tieling's chess club directly, instead taking a detour to Jia Wuhu's quadrangle. He stopped in front of the gate and found the yard gloomy and bleak. Spider webs covered the gate, as if the estate had never been cared for. Rou Rou knocked on the door, without answer. A thousand worries occupied his mind. He saw the 'Double happiness' motif ripped and discarded on the ground. The red lamps were not illuminated, and nobody seemed to be inside.

Rou Rou opened the door and found the courtyard empty. He had an ominous feeling. Sparrows swirled around bare tree branches, chirping loudly at the intrusion. He hurried down the path and rushed into his sister's room. He found the door was ajar. Inside he found his sister had hung herself.

He hurried to untie the linen cloth and lay his sister on the bed. Pain racked his heart. Tears blurred his vision, whilst he hysterically called her name. He knew this was in vain, as she was already blue and cold to touch. Rou Rou was overwhelmed with unfathomable grief. She was the only thing that made sense in his confused life. She was the only person who had cared for him.

He dried his eyes and dragged her body out into the yard and took her to a spot where he thought she would like. He buried his sister with love and reverence. He used a stone to write a tablet with the following words: *My beloved sister, Rou Feifei, whose beauty and kindness would impress the whole world if given the chance.* After gently placing the tablet on her grave, he stood up and slowly walked back to the *Plum Valley Chess Club*. His thoughts were with his sister, and he hoped that the words carved on the tablet would never fade, neither in the wind nor in a storm.

ঔ ঔ ঔ ঔ ঔ ঔ

Later, it was discovered that Rou Zengnan had used arsenic to get rid of Jia Wuhu and anyone else who tried to steal the manual. Applied to the skin or inhaled it was fatal. Rou Zengnan used his innocent and plain daughter Feifei as a piece in the 'chess game'. He knew she would blurt out the supposed whereabouts of the manual. In order to forestall any attempt to steal the precious manual, he replaced the real manual with a fake one, and had the poison smeared on each page. It was unfortunate that Jia Tianjing had not touched the pages.

Earlier that night, after the debacle with the manual, Jia Tianjing rushed back to his residence in a panic, going directly to his wife's room. She stared at him in horror. Her female intuition read his murderous instincts, yet she felt no concern.

He wanted to strangle her thin, goose-like neck, letting out a stream of curses and profanity at her, "You conspired with your father to kill me and my father!"

She took a step back, "What do you mean? You didn't get *your* treasure book?" Ha-ha, she quietly laughed to herself, but to him said, "You're pathetic. Useless as a thief, and useless as a husband, useless in bed. A bastard who wanted to steal my father's treasure." This was the first time Rou Feifei had raised her voice and fought back, as she knew that her time was over.

"You bitch! Don't you dare speak to me like that! You are no better than a whore. You don't come from a decent family, but from a thieves' den. My father is dead. Your father killed him."

"Killed him? I know nothing of this. I told you what I know. Unless they planned for me to hear that conversation." Rou Feifei's eyes opened wildly, not caring anymore.

"Liar! All women are liars! You make me sick! You have a choice. Either end your life by your own hand, or I will sell you to a brothel." With that he stormed out. She collapsed on the bed.

After he slammed the door and was gone, Rou Feifei became deadly calm. She recalled the tragic childhood she had. Once, as a child she asked her mother, "Is all the world as bad as this house?"

"Yes." Her mother had replied in a tragic tone.

From then on, Rou Feifei longed to escape the chains around her neck. She wished for marriage, but she never considered that her marriage would become her funeral. All the fond memories in her life ended with the death of her mother when Feifei was eleven years old. Only her brother warmed her heart. But he was like a servant to their father, and she could not worry about him now.

She looked at the long linen cloth on the bed. Her eyes were hollow. She felt the white cloth already around her neck, like a long white snake, soon to strangle her. She felt dizzy and hot. Her mind flashed to her father's ruthless scheming and plotting. He will destroy everyone, including himself. The secret book, the secret book! All the people wanted was that secret book. But what were they fighting for? Just a drifting cloud, which claims to hide treasure? Why did people always desire more than they needed? If they have one thing, they crave another. People were dying because of the book. And now so was she. How many more human beings are going to die from now on because of that book?

Rou Feifei gave a shrill laugh. *Death! Such an easy thing. Just close my eyes and whisper goodbye.*

With these thoughts, standing on a chair, Rou Feifei threw the long piece of white linen over the roof beam and tied it securely. Calmly, as if dressing for some happy event, she wrapped the other end of the linen around her neck, a soft scarf to caress her neck. She tied another knot. Then, without hesitation kicked the chair from under her. For a few seconds she smiled, then died without struggle.

Earlier, Jia Tianjing hurried to pack his things. He went to the *Kun Chess club* whose master was once a friend of his father. Tianjing hoped to find shelter there. Rou Feifei's laugh echoed in his ears, making his flesh creep. Was she mad? He cast a few uneasy glances at her room before he left. In anger, he tore the Double Happiness motif to pieces.

On the way to the *Kun Chess club*, Jia Tianjing wondered if his wife would kill herself – it did not seem to matter.

Wang Wengfeng was in no hurry to do harm to Jin Tieling. Now that he had Rou Rou's help, his aim was just to keep him fooled while he waited to see if the young man was trustworthy. When the time came, he would order Rou Rou to lead a riot against the *Plum Valley Chess Club*.

Rou Rou was punctual for every meeting with Wang Wengfeng. This behaviour pleased the new master. After spending each day at the *Plum Valley Chess Club*, he would go to the *Happiness Chess Club* at around four in the afternoon to report to his new master. "Today, quite to my surprise, Jin Tieling taught us a strategy once considered lost. It looks as if the sun arose from the west today, as he's never taught us these things before."

Wang Wengfeng drank his tea leisurely while listening to Rou Rou's report. Wang Wengfeng wondered what was in the first volume of the manual. He thought he would never find out because Jin Tieling never exposed the methods from the manual. Jin Tieling remained modest, unwilling to show off these skills in competition, even though he had a high reputation. Why suddenly did he now expose these strategies to the students and therefore the public? That was unlike him. There could be only two explanations, either he really wanted to boost his chess club, or the book had been stolen and he was teaching it to reduce the thief's power.

"Was it good? I mean the chess strategy." Wang Wengfeng asked.

Rou Rou shook his head, and said grudgingly, "Not really. He told me I had to go and sweep the courtyard. He pretended to be generous, but we all complained that he had hidden the best chess strategy from us until now. We all believed that Jin Tieling hid something away from us because he was afraid his disciples would become better than him and grab his golden bowl."

Wang Wengfeng laughed, "Do you want to have a game with me?"

"Of course." Rou Rou's eyes flashed with brightness. This, though, was another mask of his — in reality, he did not particularly like chess. He only played it as a child as a way to gain his father's approval. And now he played to try and gain notoriety.

Wang Wengfeng moved the 3rd pawn as his opening, to observe Rou Rou's first move and make a judgement of Rou Rou's ability at the same time. According to general chess strategy for that opening move, Rou Rou should have moved a cannon under his 7th pawn, rather than using the central Cannon to charge at the opponent directly. Wang Wengfeng's second move was to move an elephant, maintaining a defensive strategy to test Rou Rou. This confused Rou Rou, for Jin Tieling had taught him to attack aggressively, rather than losing the initiative in the beginning and allowing others to attack first.

Rou Rou was such an experienced spy that he spared no effort to get to the bottom of what Wang Wengfeng was doing, as he knew it may lead him closer to the second half of the manual. Rou Rou played according to what Wang Wengfeng expected, moving the pieces randomly. Wang Wengfeng observed Rou Rou's disorderly play and concluded that Rou Rou was not very good, lacked basic skills, but had some potential, which was exactly what Rou Rou wanted to convey.

"I can see that Jin Tieling taught you very little," said Wang Wengfeng, though he felt a little suspicious as this was quite unlike Jin Tieling's character.

"He taught much more to the other disciples, but neglected me. I don't know why," Rou Rou clutched his fist with his other hand, and said with a downcast look, acting as if he hated Jin Tieling, "He is such a careless master."

"You poor boy."

"Maybe he has worries. Jin Tieling seems to be tight with money."

"What?" Wang Wengfeng was confused. "From what I've heard his club attracts many visitors."

"Yes, but Jin Tieling does not charge students fees."

Wengfeng indicated that the meeting was over, "Tomorrow, please come on time. I have something to discuss with you."

Rou Rou smiled brightly and thanked his new master.

When he had gone, Wengfeng knew the boy was lying and many questions kept revolving in his head. As far as he knew, the first volume was in Jin Tieling's hands, so how could other chess clubs know the same strategy. Perhaps the book really had been stolen?

The next day, Rou Rou said that he had nothing to report, other than the students played amongst themselves. As they sat at the chess table, Wengfeng said, "To learn chess, you need to learn how to check the king first, as this is the only way to win, and to win is the purpose of the game. There are many strategies of checkmating: the throat cutting checkmate where you kill the advisers in the middle of the palace; the four pawn rendezvous, where you block the palace, and the pawns and chariots to suffocate the king so that he had no way to escape; the horse-cannon checkmate, which checks the king with a horse and cannon by putting them in the same central position. There are many others too. Which of the game endings do you want to learn most?"

Without hesitation, Rou said, "The throat cutting check-mate."

Wang Wengfeng smiled and said, "Of course." However, he was alarmed by this traitor's choice, as he had chosen the cruellest and boldest checkmate strategy to master. The young man in front of him was not as simple as he tried to appear. He has a sheepish appearance, but the heart of a wolf.

Rou Rou learned fast, but always maintained the same expressionless face. He asked his questions humbly, as a devoted student, "Master, what if my horse is surrounded by other pieces, and there is no way to break through, what should I do?"

"That's easy. Have you read of *The Art of War*, and *The thirty-six strategies*? For example, you could use the strategy to besiege the Wei Kingdom to rescue the Zhao Kingdom. You can also set a trap for the enemy, like in the tale of the empty city. There is a legend from Three Kingdoms period. Si Mayi from the Wei Kingdom tried to attack Xi Cheng City, which was occupied by famous military strategist Zhu Geliang. However, at the time, Zhu Geliang had no fighting generals, so he opened the gates to the city and started playing the Guqin. Si Mayi was suspicious that there may be an ambush in the city, and dared not march his army inside. In this way Zhu Geliang was able to win the war, even though he was in an empty city without any troops to guard it."

"Oh." Rou Rou kept his new master's words in his mind. "Thank you, Dear Master. What I have learned here tonight was much more than what I have learned from the *Plum Valley Chess Club* in the last three years." Rou Rou sighed.

"I am flattered." Wang Wengfeng smiled reservedly. After a pause, he said, "May I ask you a question? If I asked you to do something that would ruin Jin Tieling, would you agree?"

Rou Rou felt a sense of excitement arousing in the pit of his stomach. This was exactly what he wanted, the opportunity to create confusion. "Of course, Master. Out of gratitude towards you, I am willing to plunge into a sea of flames."

"But if what I ask is against our nation's moral code, will you still do it for me?" Wang Wengfeng's eyes were piercing and seemed to penetrate Rou Rou's soul to ascertain his intentions.

But Rou Rou was impenetrable. He smiled, with his head lowered, saying firmly, "I am your obedient student. Everything you suggest of me is as it should be. I will not challenge your orders."

"If Jin Tieling was to suffer from our actions, how would you feel about the impact on his students? Do you think they would feel the same?"

"Many of his disciples complain about his negligence, and some will follow us, as long as I raise the flag."

"Good. I will let you know the plan, you just need to follow my instructions."

The next day, Rou Rou received his instructions from Wang Wengfeng. Rou Rou was told to gather a mob outside the *Plum Valley Chess Club* under the guise of being disgruntled students. This would result in the rioters filing a claim against Jin Tieling, then, with the prime minister's covert help, he would be arrested, tried, and sent to jail. "In this way, the *Plum Valley Chess Club* will be utterly ruined." Wang Wengfeng opened a draw, and took out a bag of coins, "Here is money to pay the mob. But you must make sure that neither my name nor my club's name is ever mentioned. Do you understand?"

"Yes master."

Wang Wengfeng did not trust Rou Rou, as one could ever trust a traitor. If he betrayed one master so easily, he could betray another. Wengfeng still did not know what drove Rou;

was it a desire for money or for something else? Up until now, Rou still had not made any demands.

Afterwards, Wang Wengfeng hurried to see the prime minister, to discuss with Dan Shiran how they were to defame Jin Tieling. Dan Shiran gave Wang Wengfeng his full support. Wang Wengfeng laughed out of gratitude, "I have a feeling that a big chess game is about to start in the dynasty, and it won't be on the chessboard!"

"I also have the same feeling... and I hope you are the winner," Dan Shiran chuckled.

After getting his instructions from Wang Wengfeng and leaving the *Happiness Chess Club*, Rou Rou hurried back to the *Plum Valley Chess Club* so as not to be discovered missing. He hated himself for the double-crossing role that he was playing and felt as if he were split in half. He did not understand where he could comfortably fit in — nowhere, it seemed. But he knew if he did not fight others, he would end up destroyed instead. The best defence was to attack. This was the advice his father had given him. Like chess, the sole goal of life was to win.

The only person who meant anything to Rou was his sister. He had tried to protect her from being bullied by their father, and secretly helped her when she was in need. Sometimes he was willing to disobey his father for her safety. Reflecting on the past, Rou Rou felt agonised when he thought of the death of his sister. With her suicide, he felt that he had failed her. He often thought that he should join Feifei and die silently, instead of living a joyless life. But not yet — he still needed to avenge his sister. And, of course, he wanted to get his hands on the treasure that he was fighting for. He knew that the code in the manual was no longer a secret, and with both manuals, he would be crowned the best player in the land.

CHAPTER FIFTEEN

CHAOS IN THE PLUM VALLEY CHESS CLUB

Jin Xiaomei always arose early to clean the courtyard before her father started teaching. She loved early sunny summer mornings. The tidying did not seem like work to her. She would whisper her secrets to the flowers, and drop pebbles into the pond to see how many ripples stirred the water. *Yes, all nature has a soul.* They would listen to her troubles and secrets, silently, as her best friends. Summer evenings were also pleasant, when the breeze was cooler, and the earth gave back the warmth it had accumulated during the day.

As she swept, her mind turned to love and romance. She was too inexperienced to know the difference between the two. *Did she love the son of the enemy?* Still, her father pressed her to marry the prince. *I never considered the prince's infatuation to be a serious thing. And I don't care to climb up the social ladder, as many young ladies would. I only want a peaceful life with a sense of fulfilment.* It did not help that Wang Jing's father and her own father were sworn enemies. *Life is not that simple.* Then there was Dan Si, a well-educated and distinguished lady. She did not want to come between them. *"What do you say Miss Lotus Flower? Does Jing still think I'm a boy l? Do I look that boyish? Wang Jing was either blind or stupid. Perhaps he is duping me and plays chess with me to learn about our club? Maybe it would be easier to forget Jing and accept the proposal from Prince Zhu Wenchun. But if I want to be a chess master, I must make sacrifices for the sake of chess. Oh flower, I just don't know."* Suddenly she heard the shouting of many voices. It sounds like it was coming from the classroom area. Worried, she hurried to the classroom.

There were twenty or so men armed with sticks smashing and kicking the furniture and walls with fury. They were shouting and cursing as they did so, scaring Xiaomei. The promise of looting drove them on, as they had been promised they could keep whatever they could carry. They seemed to find savage pleasure in their destruction.

Somebody even tore off the terracotta doorplate with the words *The Plum Valley Chess Club* engraved on it and smashed it on the path. Angered at the destruction of her father's life work, she rushed to meet them and shouted, "Stop! Why are you doing this?" Jin Xiaomei scanned them, not recognising anyone until she saw Rou Rou. Clearly he was leading the mob, which he had probably bribed them off the street. He made sure they arrived at a time when most of the students were not at the club. The mob ignored her, but one shouted at her, "Tell your father to come out and stop being such a chicken, hiding like a turtle in his shell. How can he call himself a master?" Another angry man shouted unintelligibly, whilst shaking his stick at the girl.

She addressed Rou Rou, "My father never mistreated you, that's why this club has such a solid reputation. I know my father treated you as a respected disciple, what on earth has come over you?"

"I want your father to apologise! He is a lair. The chess club should be closed, it is cheating its disciples. Now, checkmate!"

"How dare you!" Xiaomei's eyes were furious.

Seeing Jin Xiaomei so resolute, Rou Rou's henchmen backed-off a little. Rou Rou began to speak, trying to turn the tide again. "We want justice from you folks." He said coldly.

"Who is we? This mob that you have raised to damage us?" Then with the same irony in her tone, "Rou Rou, you have never been treated badly. Give me examples if you will. You have always been the most silent person in the club. Now you shout with thugs and sticks." Xiaomei's penetrating eyes never left his face.

"Your father always neglected me." Rou Rou lied with palpable anger in his voice.

"Huh, neglected? What rubbish. I have never seen you learn chess with any real enthusiasm. You never let your wit show in any game. Now, you put the blame on my father! What game are you playing now?" Then she looked the mob in the eye, glaring at each in turn, and said with contempt, "How much has he paid you to hurt us?" She recognised some of the men as drunks that hung around town.

Rou Rou did not want to hurt Jin Xiaomei, but the emotion of his sister's death clouded his judgement. He clenched his jaw and gave a sign for the group to advance. The rioters moved a little towards Jin Xiaomei as if she were a brick wall and not a young and delicate girl.

Zhang Zheng who heard the noise, rushed into the room and, on the seeing her imminent peril, moved to protect Jin Xiaomei, stretching out his arms to shield the girl. He was hit and fell to the ground. Bystanders watched in horror, but too afraid to intervene.

Hearing the noise, Jin Tieling rushed out. Everyone stopped, frozen. The atmosphere was heavy with anger. He felt profound gratitude to Zhang Zheng for what he did for his daughter.

The rioters stared at Jin Tieling with a mixed feeling of fear, excitement, anger, and greed. They were uncertain of what to do next. Jin Tieling stood there, resolute "How dare you cause such damage to my chess club?" Jin Tieling said with power. The mob felt a chilling wind blowing in their ears. "I shall call the authorities and have you all taken away."

Rou Rou grasped the opportunity to speak. "Ha-ha, the authorities are on their way to have you apprehended for your misdeeds."

"Misdeeds? What are you talking about?"

"Master Jin, we want justice. I am wasting my time in your chess club. These people can see the injustice of it."

"These people? I don't know these people." Then looking at them, "Why are you against me? I have always helped the community."

Then he turned to Rou Rou, "And you? Why have you roused this mob against me and my family? If you are unhappy in the club, you are free to leave. You can find yourself another master."

"Master Jin!" Shouted Rou Rou, trying to stir the mob again. "You are a traitor to the dynasty." But the mob remained silent. Jin Tieling looked at Rou Rou in surprise and frowned, "It was you who stole the manual! You are the spy in our club. Now you stir up trouble to cover your tracks. You are being very foolish."

Rou Rou seethed; his face was blazing in the early sunlight. "What rubbish you say to save yourself." There was an echo from the followers. "Liar, liar! You are a crook."

Xiaomei was not scared by what was happening, but she was angered by the false claims and the harm done to Zhang Zheng. She helped him up to see if he was badly hurt. Seeing he was okay, she turned to confront the rioters again. The mob were acting as if they were programmed by some evil hand. She stepped forward and with dignity, "Rou Rou you know that playing chess is no different to choosing the kind of life that you want to live. If you make one wrong move, you are sure to lose the whole game. Don't expect to win in the end!"

"Of course, such a young girl knows everything about life." Rou Rou said with irony. Then he cleared his throat, spat on the paving, and said distinctively, "I don't want to argue with you, we will leave it to the civil authorities!"

"Yeah!" The crowd echoed and turned round to leave for the local townhall.

Suddenly, the courtyard was empty and silent. Left in its wake was broken furniture, torn books, smashed vases, and debris strewn everywhere. Jin Xiaomei stood there, looking around, with total abhorrence. She then went to Zhang Zheng and said, "Come in and I will make you some tea and clean you up. You poor boy, taking a beating for me – thank you." She remembered that after she stood up for him when he stole the three silver coins he said he would always look out for her – and here he did just that, risking his own safety.

Wen Wen emerged to see what the commotion was. She was already in tears and nervously clutched Jin Tieling's hands for support, upon which he led her inside. Jin Tieling comforted her and said, "Life turns a full circle."

Wen Wen said, "Rou Rou is a silly man. This is not his business. Do you think it was *his* doing?"

Tieling knew that she was referring to Wang Wengfeng.

"I don't know. But I suspect that he has played a role in today's drama."

"Sorry." There was a tear in each of Wen Wen's eyes.

"Don't worry, it's not because of you. Men would never wage a real war because of a woman. Even if it was him, all of this was just an excuse." Jin Tieling patted Wen Wen's hands to comfort her.

Jin Xiaomei overheard the conversation between her parents. It confused her.

"The worst hasn't come yet." Jin Tieling said. "It is just a prelude to a bigger storm."

"Master, Rou Rou did not deny stealing *The Secret under the Mahogany tree*?" Zhang Zheng offered.

Jin Tieling nodded his head solemnly. He said, "Rou Rou, for all his time here remained almost invisible, like a shadow. Did he come just for the sake of the manual? What is the secret behind the book? And if he did steal it, why has he chosen to come again and do more harm? And why is he perfectly willing to be Wang Wengfeng's pawn? What does he want? Who is this Rou Rou?

"Xiaomei, get the copy of the chess manual you created." She nodded her head solemnly. She hurried to get it.

Zhang Zheng said goodbye, he would go home and lie down as he had a headache.

When Xiaomei returned, Jin Tieling said, "For so many years, out of deep resentment towards Wang Wengfeng, I never gave the book a closer look. What happened must be related to the manual. We must find out the clue it holds. Xiaomei, are you sure you reproduce the book according to every detail of the original?"

Xiaomei nodded yes.

Jin Tieling was satisfied. He turned over each page, amazed at his daughter's memory and attention to detail. She was such a gifted girl. Jin Tieling finished scanning the book, and found that everything seemed normal except the front and the last pages. He looked at the section of Chen Yi's poem from the Song dynasty.

*Of chess game in the **battlefield**,*
Is just a play or a drama?
If you know how to play chess,
*The movement of **chariots** and **horses***
traced back to Zhou dynasty,
*other pieces have the title of the advisors of **Han nationality**.*

"The characters *battlefield, chariots, horses*, and *Han nationality* are all highlighted."

Jin Xiaomei nodded her head in acknowledgement and said, "I also found it strange."

"In the real Plum Valley where I studied chess, there was a cave near a stream. What is strange is that the cave had a wooden gate, in front of which were two big terracotta figures in the costume of advisers of the Han dynasty. We once asked our master to let us inside, but he forbade us, saying it was used to store food and supplies. In those times, life was hard, and he warned us not to pilfer food from the cave."

"Two terracotta figures?" Xiaomei asked amazed, "Sounds unbelievable."

"Yes, but it's true. The two terracotta advisers were as tall as men. Master told us that the two guarded the cave. He said it was sacred and we should do nothing that would disturb the peace of the place."

"It's a pity that we don't have the second half of the poem." Xiaomei said with a sigh.

Jin Tieling felt embarrassed. He now knew that it was a mistake to give the second volume to Wang Wengfeng. He felt himself like a farmer who saved a wolf from hunger, only to be bitten by it. *I was too supportive of the man who I thought of as my friend.*

"Father, do you remember the second half of the Chen Yi's poem?"

Tieling sighed, "I read it at the time, but it was a long time ago. I'll do my best to remember." He took a bamboo scroll and brush, and thought before he wrote on the paper:

> *The general plays an important role:*
> *To remove or appoint the three armies.*
> *Troops cross the river,*
> *moving quietly with stealth.*
> *A frown emerges on my face as I look back…*
> *I laughed at myself,*
> *Every chess game is a trifle of vanity.*

"What a poem!" Jin Xiaomei sighed. "The poet has far-reaching notions, implying wining or loosing is not important at all in his eyes. Because life is full of ups and downs, it's natural that we may lose the game, so it is equally natural if we win. We should just take it as it comes."

"I can't be sure it's accurate, but which lines appeal the most?" Jin Tieling asked his daughter.

"The last one, *every chess game is just a trifle of vanity.*"

"Yes, Xiaomei, what does winning mean to us?"

Jin Xiaomei pondered and said, "It means everything, but at the same time, it means nothing."

"That's it. It's a pity we don't know which characters are highlighted in the second half of the poem.

Tieling noticed a faraway look in his daughter's eyes, "What are you thinking of?" he asked, knowingly.

"Nothing." she responded solemnly.

A few hours later, a group of officers from the local constabulary stormed into the *Plum Valley Chess Club*. Without providing any explanation, they searched the entire club and confiscated anything left of value.

Jin Xiaomei hurried to burn her copy of *The Secret under the Mahogany tree* to ashes, then she swiftly returned to the courtyard. She was shocked by what she saw. What the rioters did not trash, the venal officers did. The valuable classical books were torn up and dumped causally on the ground by the heartless intruders. All the chess boards and pieces were thrown into the pond. They even trampled many of the plants in the courtyard. There was no life left in the *Plum Valley Chess Club*. The fish in the ponds stayed still in the water, as if they too were dead.

The Jin family stood frozen, stunned by this senseless destruction. None spoke, but all determined that these officers had been bribed to destroy with savage pleasure. Xiaomei tried to come to terms with the fact her family was ruined. This was the so called 'irresistible force'.

Jin Tieling watched the desecration with cold eyes. He despised those people who had no knowledge of chess, and who failed to value the wisdom left by the ancestors. All they could do was to defile those who they thought were superior too them. His lips trembled as he surrendered all hope of defending himself, bracing himself for all consequences, including being sent to jail.

When the officers found nothing left to smash or carry off, they seemed disappointed. Waving an order in Jin Tieling's face, they bound his hands with rope. The commanding officer smiled sarcastically as he scoffed, "Sorry, Master of the famous *Plum Valley Chess Club*. I am afraid that you are going to jail… for a long time." And with that, they led him to the local jail.

Jin Tieling did not respond, nor did he fight back. He went meekly, with his back straight and his head high. Wen Wen partially collapsed onto Xiaomei. Xiaomei wanted to follow their oppressors, but instead she remained behind to support her mother.

After Xiaomei lay her mother on her bed, she instructed her to rest while she went to the townhall and try to determine the reason for this madness. Wen Wen was too flustered to resist.

Arriving at the civic building, she found the main door closed. Jin Xiaomei knocked the giant door knocker with great force, but no one answered. She kept knocking hard, and shouting, "Unfair! Unfair!" Curious people were attracted by the clatter.

Finally, the door pushed opened with a noisy squeak. A pompous official looked enquiringly at her with a raised eyebrow. Yawning, he demanded, "Girl, why are you knocking so hard? It's lunch time. You can be heard all over town."

"Sir, my father was arrested unfairly this morning. He is innocent." She spoke with moderation as she knew she could not argue or agitate if she was to gain his assistance.

Again, the local pen-pusher yawned as he spoke. "Oh?"

"My father has a legally registered chess club and runs his business honestly..."

Although he fully knew which club she referred to, he asked as if bored, "What is the name of your father's chess club?"

Jin Xiaomei hated being interrupted, but she still showed respect, "It's *the Plum Valley Chess Club*, sir."

"Ah, a famous chess club that has fallen into dishonest ways."

"My father is slandered by his enemies."

"If you think your father has been treated unjustly, I will be sure to look into this matter. You need not worry. We will however need to hear all the evidence from the witnesses. I will open an enquiry."

❧ ❧ ❧ ❧ ❧ ❧

At the same time, Jia Tianjing, now safely in the *Kun Chess Club*, told the master of *Kun Chess Club* that there was probably some treasure hidden in the Plum Valley. He wanted to expose the secret of the treasure to create chaos. That way he may be able to get more people to seek the treasure with him. He told his host about how Rou Zengnan stole the first volume of the book from Jin Tieling and gave it to his father, and how he himself was tricked into a marriage with Rou Feifei, and how his father was poisoned to death when exploring the treasure book. All he wanted now was to seek revenge on Rou Zengnan.

He told his host that the treasure meant nothing to him, but that was to hide his desire to obtain it for himself. The master of *Kun Chess Club* was once a friend of Jia Tianjing's father, so he gave Jia Tianjing hospitality without reservation. It pleased him to know that there existed a chess manual that hinted at there being treasure. Jia Tianjing analysed the circumstances together with the Kun master, and they concluded that Jin Tieling must know the secret. The next person who probably knew the secret was Wang Wengfeng, who probably also held the second volume. However, here there was a problem, as Wang Wengfeng was a tough figure to deal with due to his numerous connections with top officials. So, they made their minds up to spread the news to the public, arousing in the local people's greed and desire to find the treasure, and possibly provoking them to fight for the treasure in a dog-eat-dog manner. Fishing in the troubled waters, they may find out where the volume of the book was hidden. Jia Tianjing retained a secret smile, now he knew how he would avenge his father.

So, the news was leaked as agreed. People could never resist the temptation of finding treasure and becoming rich. But when they heard that Jin Tieling's property was confiscated and he was arrested, all were shocked by the news. "It must be Rou Rou's doing." They thought.

❧ ❧ ❧ ❧ ❧ ❧

Xiaomei had no choice but to return home, waiting for the slow wheels of justice to grind towards a court appearance. She spent this time trying to clean up the mess the rioters and police had caused, and repair what she could. Some locals came to help. Wen Wen had rallied and cleaned inside the kitchen, which had been ravaged. Now over the initial shock, she knew she had to remain strong and maintain a clear head.

The day of the court case finally arrived. There were many spectators, mostly people from the neighbourhood, other business owners, and Jin Tieling's students. They were surprised that their master was facing a lawsuit, as he had always had a good and honest reputation and was kind to others. They hoped to be given the chance to testify as to his innocence. Also in the gallery were members of the mob who had been given an additional amount of money to stir things up. Some were obviously drunk.

The administrator of the court called for silence as he read out the charges of 'dishonesty and theft'. The official then addressed Jin Xiaomei, "Jin Xiaomei, you said your father is innocent. What evidence do you have for this?"

"He was arrested without reason. Everyone in town knows my father for his good reputation. Ask all these people in the gallery, they are here to support him..." Immediately the thugs started shouting, "Lies, lies."

"Silence!" the official shouted. Xiaomei continued, "My father is an advanced chess master and has devoted his life to his students. My Lord, can you tell me on what grounds the government trashed our chess club and arrested my father? If he has broken the law, we have not been told about it."

"Trashed your chess club... No... surely you exaggerate. Our officers are law abiding citizens. Anyway, a complaint has been lodged by some of your father's students. They have a different story." The local pen-pusher clapped his hands, and said drowsily, "One of your father's disciples has claimed that your father defrauded his fees without teaching him anything."

"That's nonsense. Ask my father's other students to put up an arm up if they were badly treated."

Half a dozen arms went up, but the official simply ignored them. The rabble-rousers shouted. Xiaomei shouted in agitation, "These people are not members of our club. Ask those people, sitting over there. They are our students."

The bureaucrat did not pay attention to Jin Xiaomei's defence. "We have witnesses. They will have their say soon enough." This went back and forth for some time, until the pompous official, with a frown, said, "I have heard your defence. You have proven nothing."

Next, Rou Rou was led into the court. With his lowered head and displaying not the slightest bit of emotion, he was told to state his case. In a pitiful voice, Rou Rou moaned, "My lord, As one of Jin Tieling's students, I charge him of defrauding my fees. He neglected his teaching, and I have learned nothing from him."

At these words, the agitators moaned aloud in disgust, "Shame, shame."

"Rou Rou, you have been a student of Jin Tieling at the *Plum Valley Chess Club* for three years?"

"Yes."

"But now you have found a new master, Mr Wang Wengfeng of the *Happiness Chess Club*, haven't you?"

"Yes, correct... And a fine master he is." Rou Rou said.

"Why did you leave the *Plum Valley Chess Club*?"

"Because I learned nothing at Jin Tieling's club." Rou Rou glared at Jin Tieling with an intense dislike. Again, the rabble-rousers moaned their disapproval.

"But Jin Tieling and his daughter said you seemed to have no real interest in chess."

"No. They are lying, I love chess."

"Yes, I am sure."

"Jin Tieling also beat me with a stick, as if I were a slave."

Xiaomei shouted, "Liar!" but she could not be heard over the jeering of the mobsters, "Shame, shame!"

At this moment, Jin Tieling noticed a man sitting, observing, from behind a curtain. Jin Tieling thought it looked like Wang Wengfeng. He could see that this case was proceeding like a runaway carriage, and there could only be one result. Guilty. There was a mighty hand behind this, it could be Wang Wengfeng! Or the Prime Minister himself!

The official nodded his head to the man behind the curtain with deep respect, and then turned to Rou Rou, "Why did you take three years to leave Jin Tieling's chess club?"

Rou Rou said in his whiney voice, "I have always respected Jin Tieling as my master, trying to be a good student, but he ignored my existence. I kept a low profile, humbly trying to learn. I lived on his premises, and he would lock me away so I would not escape."

"That's appalling," the official said as he glared at Jin Tieling. The mob sighed in horror. "Is there anything else?"

"Yes, Jin Tieling hid proper techniques from us. It was not until recently that he started to teach real strategy. It opened my eyes, and at the same time, I realised what he was doing. Not long ago, I watched a game between him and Jin Xiaomei, his daughter. Otherwise, I would still be in the dark. God knows the reason why he suddenly decided to teach us these advanced tactics. I feel that we have wasted so much precious time in his club."

Jin Xiaomei felt a knot in her stomach and asked if she could reply to this allegation. The official replied that she had her chance to talk earlier, and that she must now remain silent.

Jin Tieling gave Rou Rou a shocked look but said nothing. He would rather defend himself with the truth than fight back with hatred. Xiaomei was about to shout but was interrupted by the mob. Every time she tried to speak she was shouted down.

The official held up his hands for silence and turned to Jin Tieling. "You have heard of the manual known as *The Secret under the Mahogany tree?*"

"Yes, and..." But the official cut him off with, "Do you admit that you have had this manual in your possession?"

"I did, but..." Again, he was cut off.

"You stole this manual from Wang Wengfeng, who was given *The Secret under the Mahogany tree* by his master for prosperity so that it would not be exploited."

"That is not..." This time he was shouted down by the agitators, and again the official called for silence.

"You went against your master's wishes for the manual and you stole it." This time there was shouting from everyone. Once it quietened down, having got what he wanted, the official cleared his throat. Without waiting to hear any more evidence, for he wanted to wind up the case as soon as possible, he announced, "The verdict is clearly, guilty. Jin Tieling will be sent to prison for ten years!" The agitators cheered and shouted, "Justice prevails."

With these words, Jin Tieling was forced to kneel, pressed heavily down by officers. But even kneeling, his majestic air was able to silence all the people watching him. He kept his dignity. It was clear that Wang Wengfeng wanted to ruin him, and it was a waste of time to defend himself in front of such high-powered plotters.

To everyone's surprise, Jin Tieling did not attempt to defend himself further, but his expression of horror was obvious. Xiaomei wanted to defend her father but was stopped by his meaningful look. Xiaomei felt as if her world had collapsed. *How could this happen! Greedy folks turn law into thievery when it suits them.* The official had only one thought, and that was to sentence her father to jail. With Wang Wengfeng's support, and with prime minister's connections, it was a hopeless situation. How could her father have a chance against the weight of these powerful influences? The big fish were eating the small fish. Jin Xiaomei suspected that even if her father were released, the reputation of the *Plum Valley Chess Club* would be ruined – Xiaomei's father was a ruined man, without honour. How could he bear such trauma at his age!

She was about to go and confront Wang Wengfeng but was stopped by Zhang Zheng, who suddenly rushed into the court. He indicated that Xiaomei look outside. She saw a luxurious coach parked immediately by the front door. Because of the turmoil in the court, no one had noticed its arrival, but now the coach attracted the attention of onlookers. People realised something interesting was about to happen.

The person sitting in the carriage did not reveal his face. His footmen sat still on top of the carriage, looking straight ahead.

Zhang Zheng addressed himself to the official. "Sir, why have I not been brought forth to testify? I put my name down as a witness. I can vouch that master Jin Tieling never squandered the fees received from us. He is a good master, who not only taught us how to play chess, but also taught us how to be responsible citizens. Except one." he said this as he looked at Rou Rou. "He was a father to us, to those who showed interest in chess. For one as dumb as a piece of wood, who never uttered a word in the chess club, it would have been better to give up. Unless, of course, he had nefarious reasons for remaining... Nor did he practice chess with his fellows as the master asked him to do. Instead, he would sit in the corner, gazing at the waxing of moon and blossoming of flowers, as if learning chess was the most boring thing in the world."

The pompous jackass of an official was greatly annoyed by the sudden intrusion of Zhang Zheng. He was making it complicated, when all he wanted to do was to fill his belly and have his afternoon snooze. What concerned him though — and concerned Wang Wengfeng — was the identity of the man in the coach. It was obvious that the owner was a man of status, but who was he?

The townhall official felt befuddled, unable to decide what to do. However, since he had already declared Jin Tieling guilty, he was unwilling to change his verdict, especially with so many people watching. He hardened his heart, and said in a voice that was almost shrieking, "Your testimony shall not be accepted. The session is adjourned. Guards, take Jin Tieling to prison and clear the court." While he said this, he gave a surreptitious smile to Wang Wengfeng, who nodded his head slightly.

"Who dares to trample the sacred laws of the dynasty?" A loud and commanding voice came from the coach. There was much gesticulating and whispering from the crowd. Stepping out of the coach was a grand looking and well-dressed young gentleman. He was wearing a purple silk gown. On the back there was a five-clawed dragon, which reflected his title and social status. He was of a royal blood. Everyone kowtowed.

This man coming out of the carriage was no other than Prince Zhu, the man who Jin Xiaomei ruthlessly refused to marry.

It later emerged that when the court session had started, and was so obviously one-sided, Zhang Zheng had snuck out and rushed to seek help from Prince Zhu Wenchun as perhaps their last hope. When he arrived, the young prince was fortunately in his residence. Zheng asked the servant to tell the prince that a great injustice was being perpetrated on Jin Tieling of the *Plum Valley Chess Club* by the court. Would he please step out to see him? Within a few minutes Prince Zhu Wenchuan burst out, and loudly admonished to Zheng, "Dear sir, this had better not be a ruse to see me. Tell me all!"

Zheng did, telling him everything including how the manual had been stollen, the rioting, and the police raid. Then he told him of the debacle of the court case. Hearing such news, Zhu Wenchun turned pale. He told his servant to bring the carriage out front, for they must quickly go to the civic centre. They headed to the court in a great hurry. Whilst travelling Zheng, filled in more detail.

One of the current emperor's desires was to eliminate corrupt officials. The young prince was entrusted with this task and would ensure that it happened in this case.

The coach had been there for some time before Zheng came in as the prince had wanted to witness the proceedings for himself. After some fifteen minutes, he sent Zheng in to testify, and saw the rejection of his testimony by the official. There must be collusion between the businessman sitting behind the curtain and the government official. From what Zheng told him, and what he observed, it all came down to this Rou Rou character. When he heard the official announcing the end of the case, he became indignant and spoke out.

As he entered the court room, many bowed their heads. He was imperious as he confidently strode forward, overshadowing everyone. Even Jin Xiaomei was deeply impressed by the determination of Zhu Wenchun. He stopped in front of the official, without taking his glare from him. The pompous official was scared out of his wits. In his imperious voice, which was raised so all could understand his intention, he raged, "How can you deliver a sentence to a man without hearing all the evidence?"

The onlookers saw the pants of the official become damp. They giggled. The official, not so pompous now, said in a trembling voice, with his knees too weak to stand up, "I am sorry. I have made a terrible mistake in judgement, My lord." He said this with his head bowed.

Then the young prince turned to Wang Wengfeng and said, "And, who are you? I demand you come out from that curtain." Wang Wengfeng did so, and kowtowed to the prince, "I am Wang Wengfeng, My Lord. I..." But without waiting for an answer the prince continued, "It is you who has accepted this young man — what's his name? Ah, Rou Rou — as your disciple?"

Wang Wengfeng nodded his head coldly but modestly. He knew this young man was the son of the royal prince, and had a reputation for being well-versed in civil affairs. Rumour had it that this Zhu Wenchun was especially favoured by the emperor because of his integrity and keen mind. In the court, this young, strong-minded man usually held a different opinion on national affairs to that of the prime minister. Dan Shiran once spoke about this Prince Zhu with Wang Wengfeng and complained about the emperor's obvious fondness for this young prince.

"Yes. I have accepted him as my disciple." Wang Wengfeng said with false calm.

"Is it true that you and Jin Tieling were friends, when you both studied chess in the Plum Valley?"

"Yes, we were."

"So, if I remember well, both of you are the direct disciples of Wang Siyi?"

"Yes, we are."

An idea occurred to Prince Zhu Wenchun. "I shall deal with this in a moment." He then asked, his eyes sparkling with curiosity, "Whose skills are superior? Yours or Jin Tieling's?"

"When we were in the Plum Valley, we were equal." Wang Wengfeng said reluctantly. He disliked anybody dragging out memories from the past.

"Oh, so you haven't played chess with each other since then?"

"No."

"Can both of you be called the two greatest chess players in the current dynasty?" He said this whilst looking at Jin Tieling. Tieling answered, "It's hard to say. There are many chess masters in China, and of course there are endless games to play. There are mountains behind mountains, and people behind people."

"Well, I have a declaration. Since the founding emperor Zhu Yuanzhang announced the grand chess contest to gather all chess players throughout the dynasty, we have not had another chess contest. We are going to hold a second chess contest. All the chess clubs of the dynasty will be invited to send representatives to take part. We will see who is number one at the end of the competition. What do you think of this idea?" He cast a passing glance at the audience. All the onlookers were enthusiastic. They started applauding and cheered. The idea of organising another grand chess contest in the current dynasty was novel and exciting.

The prince turned his attention to Rou Rou, "And you, do you think it is a good idea?"

Rou Rou was shocked to be spoken to directly by the prince. He stammered, "Yes, Your Highness."

"And will you compete?"

For the first time in three years, Rou Rou made a mistake. Perhaps it was the loss of his sister, or the pressure of the court case, who can say? But with enthusiasm, he replied, "Yes, I will... and I will win it."

"Indeed, are you good enough to win?"

Rou Rou immediately realised his mistake.

The prince mocked him, "Oh, if you are good enough to win, then surely your master... your real master, Master Jin Tieling, has taught you well. Would you not agree?"

Rou Rou had lost his voice.

The prince was relentless, "Speak... boy. Tell the truth. But before you open your mouth, consider the consequences of lying in a civil court. Did your master teach you or not?"

"Yes, he did." was all Rou Rou could squeak.

"And, who put you up to this crime of denouncing your master?"

Rou Rou turned and looked at Wang Wengfeng for guidance. The answer was obvious.

The prince looked at Wang Wengfeng, "Remembering the punishment for lying. You sir... is there any reason why you should not pay all the costs for the full repairs to the *Happiness Chess Club?*"

Wang Wengfeng, incensed with anger, squeaked out a "No."

"Speak up Mr Wang. I can't hear you."

Wang Wengfeng stammered "Ye-yes, I will pay for the repairs."

"It would seem," announced the prince, "that based on this court official's admission of inept civil procedure, the admission from this young boy of wrong-doing, and by the acknowledgement of Mr Wang, it is obvious that there has been a grave injustice. I dismiss this court. Mr Jin is free to go. And you sir," he now readdressed the official, "you are relieved of your position. You shall never work in the emperor's administration again." There was a great cheer from the court participants.

When the crowd had quietened down, the prince announced, "The date of the contest shall be on the Mid-Autumn festival, about one month from now. I will order the officials to place an announcement throughout the dynasty. And..." he paused for affect, "women will be invited to play, should they want to."

Everyone kowtowed, as he walked out of the court.

Zhu Wenchun ignored Jin Xiaomei as he passed by her, neither looking at her nor acknowledging her. He then ascended into his coach, which rolled away in grand style.

Jin Tieling returned home to find his students waiting anxiously at the gate. When they saw their master coming, there was a cheer. However, Jin Tieling was in no mood to continue the business of the chess club at that time. He spoke to his disciples and told them the club will be closed for a month to complete the repairs. After what Jin Tieling had experienced, he was exhausted. The students cried out "We will never go; we will help you repair the club. You are our master!"

CHAPTER SIXTEEN

THE MEETING IN THE CONFUCIAN TEMPLE

Xiaomei went to see her mother after the court case to check she was okay. When she opened the door, she was surprised to see her mother shedding tears in front of the copper mirror. Xiaomei was at a loss as to what to say, nor did she know how to comfort her mother. Approaching her she said in a clumsy way, "Father is safe. He has been released from jail. And Mother, the good news is that Wang Wengfeng has been ordered to pay the costs for all the repairs. It turns out he was the one behind this."

Hearing this, Wen Wen murmured whilst staring at the floor, "It's my fault. It is all my fault." "What are you talking about?" Xiaomei was confused.

Wen Wen held the old handkerchief in her hands and unfolded it. Xiaomei saw the two love birds vividly embodied. The golden silk was worn after all these years. "Mother. What is this?!"

Wen Wen said, "Sit down Xiaomei there are things I have to tell you." She then related the entire story of how she met her father and Wang Wengfeng, and what had happened next. Xiaomei guessed that deep in her heart she still had space for Wang Wengfeng, even after all these years.

What surprised Xiaomei most was that for all these years her father had treated her mother with respect, putting it behind him. Wen Wen had buried Wang Wengfeng's name in the bottom of her mind, afraid to touch the scar, but she was still unwilling to throw the handkerchief away. Her parents respected each other greatly, and her father had never played with any other women.

Wen Wen gave Xiaomei a searching look, full of doubt and suspicion, afraid to be looked down upon by her own daughter. Xiaomei's smile reassured her.

"Mother, it's not your fault. You had no control over your life. Wang Wengfeng would hate Father even without your existence. Just ease your mind and rest. The problem will be solved." Xiaomei smiled.

Wen Wen said, "This handkerchief was embroidered for Wang Wengfeng, but your father gave it back to me and proposed to me. He is a good man and I love him."

"Mother, you have been fretting too much. Stop blaming yourself. Since ancient times, women's fate has been sealed by man and God. Beautiful women are always an object of envy, and it is even worse for talented women."

Afraid to add more to her mother's worries, the daughter offered a bright smile, "I don't see any reason for you to feel ashamed of your past."

Hearing this Wen Wen felt relieved.

Having cheered her mother up a little, the girl left the room. As she came out, she passed her father, who suddenly said to Xiaomei, "I think Prince Zhu Wenchun is still in love with you. You see how he could not trust himself to look at you in the courtroom as he departed?"

Xiaomei did not want to discuss it with her father, so she just smiled and said, "Perhaps." After what she'd heard from her mother, she needed some time to herself and went to the pond. There were so many things she wanted to straighten out in her mind. She could not forget the look of envy on Wang Wengfeng's face as he stared at her father in the courtroom. Xiaomei felt a pang in her heart when she realised the old resentment from her father's generation was too tricky to solve. The fact that Wang Jing was the son of Wang Wengfeng created complexities. And then there was Prince Zhu Wenchun. She was worried about her father pushing her to marry him – she would not sacrifice her passion for anyone. Then her mind was haunted by the ugly image of Rou Rou and his conniving, and a sense of disgust overpowered her. It all gave her a headache.

It started to rain. She looked up to the sky and opened her mouth to catch raindrops. She could no longer distinguish between her tears and rain. Although it was cold, she did not notice. Xiaomei knew that the carefree days of her teenage years were over. Responsibility descended on her shoulders like a large rock. She felt as if her heart was being torn to pieces, and she had no one to share her secret with. She had only the raindrops and lotus flowers for company. Reason finally came back to her – now was not the time for melancholy.

Xiaomei walked aimlessly down the street, the light rain blurring her vision. She mingled with the crowd, trying to hide her concerns on her face. She considered the chess contest. *Yes, a chess contest. I will play and do my best.*

She tried to recreate the image of Zhu Wenchun in her mind, and decided that it was unlikely that she would ever love him. Life was like this. If the people on the street knew what she was thinking, they would be sure to laugh at her, *for a girl who was born into a common family, was it not enough for her to marry into royalty? What else does she want? In her wildest dream, a sparrow could never be a phoenix. But why did she meet and fall in love with Wang Jing, while they were the children of sworn enemies?*

Realising she had reached the Confucian temple, she paused at the gate and decided to wander inside. It was quiet, though a lot of worshipers were burning incense sticks, and most were praying silently. The rain for now had stopped. She followed the worn stone path into the temple. She took an incense stick from a vendor and started to pray. Her first wish was to pray for the good health of her parents; second was to have the chess club be a place of support for the students. Her last prayer was to find luck in love, and to leave her ancestors to unravel her love live.

Having finished her prayers, she got up to leave. She passed by the large bell in the middle of the temple. A young devotee was knocking the bell. He did this ten times, whilst praying for students to have an auspicious result in the Imperial exam. Such evening drums and mornings bells reverberated in this busy town.

Xiaomei stepped outside and wandered to a tall tree where ribbons hung with love-knots. Fate would have it that Dan Si was tying love knots on this pine trees. She was intent on tying with exceptional love, whispering some prayer at the same time. She was wearing a light green coloured upper garment, and white coloured dress, which was made of delicate material. Xiaomei was wearing a coarsely cut working dress, red in colour. She knew she looked inferior, both in birth and in manner. Xiaomei blushed, and walked away as soon as possible, trying to avoid being seen.

"Miss Jin Li, please wait." she heard Dan Si's voice calling out. Xiaomei had to stop. She turned around, and with a wry smile was face to face with her rival. However, to be honest, Xiaomei had never disliked Dan Si, even if they were rivals in love.

Dan Si looked Jin Xiaomei up and down, secretly sighing and telling herself *Jin Xiaomei is a rare beauty. Her beauty is not seductive or showy, but another kind of beauty, independent and proud. Jin Xiaomei is capable of loving passionately, and willing to make sacrifices if necessary.* Dan Si said with a little jealousy, "I knew you were a girl in disguise. My silly Wang Jing is still troubled every day that he has fallen in love with a boy!"

Jin Xiaomei laughed lightly at Dan Si's humour, taking note of the '*my* Wang Jing'. She said in a soft voice, a little reluctantly, "Sorry for deceiving you, but I had no choice. If I do not disguise myself as a boy, no one would play chess with me."

"How I admire you!" Dan Si said with her usual sincerity and sweetness, "I don't play chess because I'm afraid of castigation, it being men's business. You have such courage. You dare to do something that we other women dare not try. Competing with men, staking your wisdom on the chessboard. No wonder Wang Jing adores you so much! You are so different from the rest of us."

"Ha-ha. Thank you, but there is no need to be jealous of me. It is me who should be envying you, born high, and with such looks. People like me must make our choices as best as life allows... good or bad. And then face the consequences. We endure the troubles and worries that life brings." Xiaomei said this with a smile.

"Don't say that. To be honest, I also have something rebellious and wild in my character. That's why I don't hate you, even though Wang Jing has fallen in love with you." Dan Si's eyes sparkled with girlish delight. "Maybe it is only you who deserves him and who will make him happy."

Jin Xiaomei was at a loss as to how to reply. She was surprised by Dan Si's openness, while she was so secretive. Xiaomei gave her a faint smile and concluded that Dan Si did not know anything about the resentment and hatred between Wang Jing and her father.

Si continued, "My father once told me stories about your grand master Wang Siyi. He was also courageous, and beautifully honest."

Xiaomei changed the topic and asked, "Are these lover's knots you tie to the tree?"

Dan Si smiled rather helplessly, "Yes. I don't know whether it is going to work or not."

"For Wang Jing's sake?" Xiaomei asked.

Dan Si nodded her head shyly. "I do not think it is going to do the job because he loves you, though we are engaged."

"It's impossible for us to be together." Xiaomei blurted out. She immediately regretted saying this. Then she said, "It seems that you love him so much."

"Yes, I would die for him." Dan Si said passionately. "We have known each other forever. Ever since I can recall, I have treated him as my husband-to-be."

Xiaomei comforted Dan Si and said in a sisterly manner, "Please ease your mind. I won't steal Wang Jing from you."

"Why?" Dan Si's asked intrigued, "I believe you love him too."

Xiaomei smiled and did not answer. *Why did fate play with her? She fell in love at the wrong time, and to seemingly the wrong person. Why does Wang Jing's father plot to ruin her father! It could only mean one thing: be it in the real world or on the chessboard, she had to sacrifice something in order to win, as the opening was bad. She had to struggle hard for a good ending. She would sacrifice her love for Wang Jing.* Her thoughts pained her.

"Before he met you, Wang Jing and I were good together. We almost had no secrets from one another. On one occasion, his top was torn by thorns on a bush. I mended it for him, just as a wife would. Since then, he often wears that top, unwilling to discard it." Dan Si said this with a faint smile on her face. Xiaomei smiled too, as in her eyes, all women in love looked beautiful. Again, she was jealous but deeply touched. She asked herself *could I love Wang Jing just as deeply as Dan Si does, and sacrifice everything for his sake?* She knew it to be unrealistic. *Oh, good heaven, what do I want from life?* She asked herself. The most important reason why she loved Wang Jing was because he was able to match her chess skill! That was not reason enough to take him as a husband. She heard her voice saying, "I do not want to separate you from Wang Jing."

"Why? If you love him, and he loves you, it doesn't make sense?" She was confused by Jin Xiaomei's words, while at the same time she was relieved.

Xiaomei just smiled palely and said nothing.

"Miss Jin, what is your real name? I don't believe 'Li' is your real name."

"Jin Xiaomei." Xiaomei pronounced her name in a clear voice.

"Just like you. What a beautiful name! You have the same charming trait in your personality. Just like a wintersweet flower, not afraid of a snowstorm in the cold of winter. There are not many women like you."

"Thank you, you are very kind."

"Can we be friends? Even if Wang Jing stands between us?"

"I would like that, but Wang Jing will not come between us."

They were walking and talking at the same time and arrived at a wishing well with many coins on the bottom. Dan Si said to Jin Xiaomei, "Have you heard the story about wishing wells, and how they can show your fortune?"

"No, tell me please."

"The tale has it that when you throw coins into this well, if the coins keep floating, or slowly sinks to the bottom at a diagonal, it is a good omen. It means good fortune, either with money or luck."

Xiaomei was amused by this tale. She wanted to test this and see what her fortune was to be. Dan Si, praying silently and dropped several coins in. All immediately sank. Dan Si could not help feeling downcast and sighed, "It must be a foolish superstition." Xiaomei took out a coin and dropped it into the water. It lingered on the surface much longer, before floating diagonally towards the bottom. Jin Xiaomei smiled happily. *It was a good sign. But for what?*

CHAPTER SEVENTEEN

BLOOD AND WIND IN JIANG HU

When Xiaomei arrived home she looked at the former wrecked courtyard. The students had worked tirelessly and the mess had now been completely cleared. The flowers had partially recovered, as if they had endured a heavy storm. In the classroom the broken chairs and tables had been removed and a few intact chairs had been saved. Remembering the devastation, Xiaomei felt sadness and desperation.

She walked towards her father's room and knocked on the door. She wanted to see how her father was. She heard a terse, "Come in" from inside, the same loud, and strong voice, as if he were never broken nor destroyed. This made her happy. She opened the door and saw her mother standing next to her father with one hand on his shoulder. She looked washed-out. Her father sat tall and dignified. He nodded his head to Xiaomei when she came in. Xiaomei felt a lump in her throat, but she said comfortingly, "Father, everything will turn out well. The sun will rise tomorrow as its always does. The new furniture for the students will arrive soon."

But her father was thinking about something else entirely, and immediately turned the conversation to the prince. He gave his daughter a confused look, "What a picky girl you are. Can't you feel that Prince Zhu is deeply attached to you? How dare you humiliate a prince on a whim? If you married him, you would have everything; wealth and titles. You will become the happiest woman in the world."

"Would I be happy Father? I might have wealth, but it is impossible to have titles. He would likely marry me as a concubine, and there are no titles for concubines. Not that I want any. Father, it worries me... the emperor decides everything according to his whim. When the emperor is happy all can be good. But when the emperor is displeased, even his own family get murdered. It is risky to marry a prince. The young Prince is the favourite of the emperor for now, but who knows about tomorrow? The emperor will eliminate anyone he is disgruntled with... including his family. You have read the history books and know as well as I of the fickle nature of emperors."

"Silly girl. You are talking treason! Luckily there is no nobody around to hear what you just said. Otherwise we would be beheaded, all of us."

"I'm careful. I know to weigh my words before I speak, especially in public. But that is exactly what I worry about. From me, or the prince, one wrong word and we could be eliminated. History shows that. Besides, I do not love him!"

She had other things to talk about, and tried to change the subject, "Father, do you think there is treasure in Plum Valley?"

Tieling knew she changed the topic on purpose and replied, "There could be. It could be in that cave that our master told us to keep out of, which was supposed to store food. Master Chong Xu forbade us to enter, warning that if we did, we would set off traps that were set up to prevent intruders. A little too ghastly and scary for us, so we kept away. Later, we forgot about it."

"It sounds like if there is treasure that's where it is hidden." Xiaomei mused aloud. Tieling nodded his head. "Possibly. Xiaomei."

Changing her thoughts again, "Father, are you going to play in the chess competition?"

"No."

"Why not? Don't you want to show all that you are the best chess player in the dynasty?"

"Why do I need to do that? Whether or not I am does not matter."

"Well, our chess club will earn a great reputation."

"Our chess club will gain a good name because we train players who love chess, and who are good plyers. No, I will not play. But you must. You are young, and competition sharpens one's game. But now back to the prince. You need to think of your future. You can't feed yourself with chess, even if you become a champion."

"Father, I only want to marry a man who I love. If I can't, I would rather live alone all my life. I will make the sacrifice to preserve the chess culture of the Plum Valley."

"Alas, I just can't understand. Prince Zhu is so in love with you, why can't you marry him? What you say is just an excuse."

"Father, don't say such things anymore. This is my fate, we must accept it! I am ready to take full responsibility. Do not ever mention this subject again." With these words, Jin Xiaomei left the room.

The news that *The Secret under the Mahogany tree* had a treasure code inside spread beyond the city, helped by Jia Tianjing. In the beginning, masters of the different chess clubs were suspicious about the existence of such a book, but after watching Jin Tieling's trial, they were convinced that such a treasure really did exist. Most concluded that the book was not with Jin Tieling anymore, and they wondered if Rou Zengnan had it. From then on, spies frequented Rou Zengnan's chess club looking for some hint of the book's whereabouts. Rou Zengnan laughed it off when these unwelcome visitors dared to mention it to him. He insisted that his chess skills were acquired from Wang Siyi himself, and the chess manual was given to him by the master. However, he was still worried that the book would be stolen. He was restless, especially at night. He had good reason to be concerned.

One cold, starry night, when the courtyard was quiet and the crickets chirped, Rou Zengnan had a nightmare. He dreamt that he was being pursued by dozens of people, and he was running away with *The Secret under the Mahogany tree*, which he held tight to his chest. He ran, frantic, until he fell. The villains who chased him turned into wild bears. Suddenly, his deceased daughter was waving her hands in front of him and beckoning him to come to her. He followed her voice, and ran on, but came to a deep abyss. The wild bears were still chasing him and getting closer. Frantic, he jumped into the abyss, sinking, and crying out in fear — it was then that his concubine woke him from his nightmare. He was drenched in sweat.

Later the same night, Rou Zengnan was woken again, this time not by his mistress, but by someone who was holding a knife to his neck. His concubine shrieked, and the thief gagged her mouth with an item of clothing to shut her up. Rou Zengnan wondered if this was another nightmare. The thief spoke with coldness, "Everything turns a full circle, yin and yang. Does it not?"

Although the thief wore a scarf around his face, Rou Zengnan had a feeling it was Jia Tianjing. Rou Zengnan's heart was pumping so hard he felt giddy. He managed to speak with his usual calm and cunning wit, "What do you want from me?"

"You know what I want."

"Valuables? You will find them in the bags inside the cupboard, which are near the shelf. Take whatever you can carry."

"You cunning rat. I don't want your jewellery. I want the manual and justice. Where is the manual?" The man demanded.

"So, it is you… Jia Tianjing. My so-called son-in-law. I no longer have the manual."

"If you don't tell me the truth, I'll kill you."

"If you kill me, you still won't get the manual."

"Then I will kill your beautiful concubine." With these words, the thief suddenly put the knife into his companion's throat. Blood pumped from the wound.

Rou Zengnan backed away on the bed, and in panic shouted, "I'm telling you the truth. I don't have the manual. It was stolen by Wang Wengfeng."

"Liar!" Without any further enquiry, the thief quickly plunged the knife into Rou Zengnan's heart. He died within seconds. "That is for my father." muttered the thief. He left empty-handed.

Weeks later, when Rou Rou was told his father was dead, curiously he did not shed a single tear. Instead, he continued his attempts to get the second manual and the treasure. Rou Rou went to the *Kun Chess Club*. He met Jia Tianjing, who was helping the master with the guests. When Jia Tianjing's eyes met Rou Rou's, he became alert. He suspected that Rou Rou was seeking revenge. However, Rou Rou put the chess manual on the table, and said flatly, "My father is dead. I want to form an alliance with you to find the treasure."

Jia Tianjing asked with confusion, "Why should I trust you?" but then he reminded himself, *Rou Rou does not know that I killed his father.*

"Because I am not like my father. It is because of him that my sister died, I don't blame you."

Jia Tianjing was wary. *Perhaps I'm not implicated.* He sighed, "It was a terrible thing that my wife did. I loved her dearly."

"I am sure. But back to business. We will select some helpers who are interested in finding the treasure with us. We will meet after the chess contest during the Mid-Autumn festival. Everybody will be too busy to notice we have gone."

More and more guests visited the *Happiness Chess Club*. They sought opportunities to ask master Wang Wengfeng questions. Wang Wengfeng was suspicious. He was cautious when having conversations with his guests, trying to keep his secret safe. "Have you heard of the troubles Jin Tieling is having? And what about Rou Zengnan? Someone put a knife in his heart and slashed the throat of his concubine. They were probably looking for the manual. Have you heard of a manual, *The Secret under the Mahogany tree?*" The questions kept coming from different guests.

Wang Wengfeng would say, "No, I have not."

"Ha-ha, I thought you might have. I've just heard rumours... Anyway, I hope to see you at the chess contest during the Mid-Autumn festival." One guest said, laughing drily.

Rou Rou coolly observed these happenings. His plan of spreading information had worked. Everybody watched everyone else. This meant less people watched him. He must find a way to get the second volume of the book before others got their hands on it, before the contest.

CHAPTER EIGHTEEN

THE THIRD GAME

Back in her room, Xiaomei was at a loss as to what she should do next. Never in her life did she feel so flustered and confused. She was torn between responsibility, moral code, and her puppy love for Wang Jing.

She recalled how she met Dan Si in the Confucian temple. Dan Si told her that Wang Jing still did not know if she was a girl or boy. She could not help smiling. She decided now was the time to visit the *Happiness Chess Club* for the last game, to determine if Wang Jing knew the strategy from the first manual, except this time she would dress up as a lady.

An hour later, Xiaomei looked at herself in the copper mirror. She had used her red paper to lightly colour her lips (In those times, Chinese women rubbed their lips on red infused wax paper as a form of lipstick). She finished off with white powder on her face. A pink hairpin held her long black hair up. She wore a long dress and a red cotton coat. She stole another glance in the mirror. This was the first time she had made-up so carefully. She was satisfied.

Walking towards the *Happiness Chess Club*, Xiaomei was nervous. Her mind was teeming with troubled thoughts. For a moment she compared herself with Dan Si – *Dan Si had looks and wealth. But I have greater intelligence and freedom.* But at the same time, her promise to Dan Si made her feel guilty.

Would she honour it? She thought of what her father had told her that he regretted giving the second part of the manual to Wang Wengfeng. Could she see it before it falls into the wrong hands?

She sighed. Unconsciously, she had reached the *Happiness Chess Club* and walked inside. She started looking for Wang Jing. Of course, she attracted the attention of many guests in the club, who wondered who this beauty was who dared visit a man's club. Xiaomei modestly lowered her head, keeping a low profile, and walked towards Wang Jing's room. As she looked around her, she saw Rou Rou, idle as usual. She was certain that his reason for being in the *Happiness Chess Club* was to steal their volume of the manual. As she walked into the room, she avoided being noticed by him.

"My lady. Can I help you?" A servant who held the curtain asked.

"I am looking for young Master Jing. Tell him that Jin Li has come to play."

There was a few seconds hesitation from the servant, "Very well. Please wait."

The servant left and Jin Xiaomei looked around the room. On her two previous visits she had not taken much notice of the room. It was quiet and elegantly furnished. On the walls were bookshelves filled with dusty old classics. It was more like a library than a chess room. In the middle of the room was placed a plum vase filled with flowers, arranged to embody zen spirit. It looked effortlessly simple but held a deeper meaning.

Xiaomei mused to herself that under different circumstances it could have been her and Wang Jing that would have been playmates as children, instead of him and Dan Si.

"Brother Jin, finally, you have arrived. I have been waiting for you for such a long time." Wang Jing started speaking before he entered the room. His voice was cheerful. Xiaomei heaved with a sigh of anticipation. At least he was as true to her as a friend.

As he burst in, Xiaomei smiled, meeting Wang Jing's eyes laughingly. When Wang Jing saw her, he froze. She enjoyed the spectacle, but he soon enough recovered himself with a bright smile. His days and nights of confusion were now resolved. He wanted to shake Xiaomei's hands as usual but hesitated, pondering whether or not it was proper. Instead, he rubbed his hands together awkwardly.

Xiaomei was a little embarrassed too, seeing such a natural expression of happiness from Wang Jing. She laughed generously, which immediately eased the awkward atmosphere.

Wang Jing said in a deeply emotive voice, "I should have guessed it. How could a boy be as charming and graceful as you? No boy's skin is as soft and smooth as yours. I am so stupid."

"I am truly sorry to have deceived you… but how else could I play chess? Anyway, I'm here to keep my promise and play another game with you. That is if you are still interested?" Xiaomei gave a challenging smile.

"Oh yes. Of course." Wang Jing hurried to put the pieces on the chessboard in order. The two sat on the opposite sides of the table, and Wang Jing said, "Miss Jin, you really surprised me. There is nothing for me left to say but to show my deep regards towards you. I never thought a woman could be so good at chess as you are. To be honest, I believe you could also defeat my father someday."

Xiaomei felt anxious at the mentioned of his father. She tried to not show it on her face; instead, she gave him a charming smile, "I could never consider myself on the same level as your father. But thank you for the compliment."

"Miss Jin, you are too modest."

Xiaomei smiled at the pleasantries as the game started. Wang Jing's mind was not on the game, instead his eyes fixed on her face. She blushed but focused on her reason for being there; to learn if he had absorbed the strategy of the first part of the book.

To try and pull him into the game, Xiaomei changed her usual strategy by employing the central cannon. Her obvious designs on Wang Jing's king did not go unnoticed by him. He was surprised at her early aggression. Perhaps this was just a ruse. But she was in no hurry to win, as she wanted him to have plenty of time to use the tactics from the first half of the manual.

Some twenty moves later, she applied more pressure by moving her second central cannon in the middle of the palace, placing the cannons together to check his king. Wang Jing, trying to get back into the game, could see that she had bought her best game with her today, and he could not match it. He never wanted to be beaten by anyone and so forced himself to focus. He knew her move was not decisive, but he still needed to get out of this mess. He did so by sacrificing a few pieces. He was still in with a chance. But at this moment, she was being a good warrior; a clever commander displaying both wisdom and strength. They attacked and counter-attacked, neither party giving in. But Xiaomei controlled the game from the start, until finally she captured Wang Jing's king with a strategy that he was not aware of. She won the game.

"Congratulations." he said with sportsmanship. It was not easy for him to be a loser. He stared at the chessboard, trying to work out how he had lost. Wang Jing looked at Jin Xiaomei, whose thin and slender body portrayed not the slightest trace of masculine aggression that most chess players required. She just smiled demurely, triumphant, but composed.

For her part, she could see that he had no knowledge of the first part of the manual. He hadn't seen it.

"Well done, Miss Jin. You really are a wonderful player. I feel that I have met my match."

She could see his sincerity and said, "No, you are too harsh on yourself. Our first game was a stalemate. You won the last game. So now we are even. Not now, but soon we must have the fourth and deciding game. Maybe it will be at the competition?"

"Nonsense. In the second game, I won because you were sick." Wang Jing said gallantly.

Xiaomei blushed, and for a moment she said nothing. To break the awkward atmosphere, Wang Jing laughed "Ha-ha. I don't even know your real name. Is your name really Jin Li?" Wang Jing looked at her with interest.

"No, of course not. My name is Jin Xiaomei."

"Jin Xiaomei? I know that name, but I can't remember from where..." She hesitated. This was a crucial moment, "It is because my father and your father were once companions at Plum Valley."

Wang Jing asked tentatively, "Is your father Jin Tieling?"

Xiaomei acted as if she knew nothing of their fathers' vendettas, "Yes. He is my father. It is he who taught me to play chess."

"You are from the *Plum Valley Chess Club*?"

"Yes," she said, waiting for the explosion.

"Our fathers were disciples of the master who lived in the legendary Plum Valley, which was one of the most sacred places for learning chess. He told me once his master gave him a precious chess book, *The Secret under the Mahogany tree* before he left the valley."

"Yes, I know of this book." Xiaomei said innocently, though with a stab of conscience in her stomach.

"I have only read the second volume. God knows where the first volume is, as my father never told me about it."

"Well... my father had the first volume. But it was stolen from us several months ago."

"What! And you have not got it back?"

"No. But we believe we know who took it. Time will reveal him."

Jing was quiet for a moment before asking, "I can show you our half of the book if you want? My father is not here." Wang Jing said excitedly. Then he stood up and went to one of the bookshelves near the door. Quite unexpectedly, he took out a dusty book from a middle shelf. Nobody would imagine that Wang Wengfeng would put this most valuable manual in such an exposed place.

"Before you pass the book over," she said tentatively, "Are you sure you want to show me? Because I know the first part of the book by heart..."

He shook it off and continued, "Do you know what is in our half?"

She replied, "No, only that the theme is about losing the

initiative in order to win, such as using the one-move handicap, or two if you wanted. Our half is the complete opposite, and covers how to win by gaining the initiative."

"Which one is better? Yours or mine?" He asked rhetorically. Then, as if to answer his own question, continued, "We've played three games so far. We drew in the first, I apparently won the second, and you won this time, fully showing your skills. I think it is obvious that gaining the initiative is superior to losing the initiative."

She replied, "Not necessarily, because it depends on how the player plays the game! A weak chess player who is playing a better player who is not using either strategy, is still likely to lose. But, if the weak player used the losing initiative, then they will do much better. Or last longer. So really, they are just tools, depending on the way the game goes."

"Here is the manual." He said passing it to Xiaomei. She received it with trembling hands and quickly turned over each page until she found the second half of Chen Yi's poem, which she read to herself and to confirm if it was the same as her father remembered;

> *The **general** plays an important role*
> *To remove or appoint the three armies.*
> *Troops cross the **river**,*
> *moving quietly with stealth.*
> *A frown emerges on my face as I look back…*
> *I laughed at myself,*
> *Every chess game is a trifle of vanity.*

Jin Xiaomei took note of the highlighted characters, **general** and **river**. She quickly scanned some strategies, grasping the main thrust of them without having the time to take it them-in in detail. She returned the book to Wang Jing, smiled, and said "Thank you for trusting me. When ours was stolen, I made a copy based on my memory. Although I will have to make another, as it's only fair that you get to see it."

"Thank you. That is very good of you to offer."

Xiaomei took the opportunity to ask, "What do you make of your father's new student Rou Rou? Do you know he is sitting just outside this room?"

"I don't like him. There is something sneaky about him. But my father is civil to him. Why do you ask?"

"We are convinced he is the traitor who took our volume." Wang Jing needed to consider these things and so changed the conversation by suggesting, "Let's go out and have a drink? I want to hear about your early life, learning chess with your father. We could have a drink in our bar but too many people are watching. Let's go for a stroll and find a quiet and more private place." Xiaomei nodded her head but said, "Is it safe just to put the book in the middle shelf near the door?"

"That's my father's idea. He thinks it's a good place because it is easy to reach but hard to be stolen. No thief would ever imagine we would put such an important volume in an obvious position on the bookshelf." He then laughed loudly at the simplicity of the idea.

"Your father is a genius!" she said, but remembered Rou Rou was idling by with narrowed eyed.

They roamed the streets of the old capital, shoulder to shoulder. The Qinhuai River rolled her waters slowly. In the harbour, many dragon boats waited to start a new journey or arrive from one. Along the riverside were shops, stores, restaurants, and entertainment venues. Singers could be heard, their voices fading the further they went, just like a stone thrown into the depth of the river, slowly vanishing in the river of time.

Xiaomei said, "I don't feel like a drink in a bar."

"Sure. What do you want to do?" Wang Jing smiled and tilted his head.

"Let's just sit on a bench by the riverside and watch the sunset." She felt tired, both physically and mentally, and wanted to tell Wang Jing everything that had happened recently. But she could not open her mouth, as she felt there was a huge gap between Wang Jing and her, one which was hard to close.

"Very well," he agreed as they sat down. They silently watched the dark curtain descending from the sky as a three-quarter round moon made its way above the horizon. The reflections of the houses along the riverside diminished, and a breeze blew ripples across the water.

She felt a twinge of pain in her heart. *Why can't this beautiful moment last longer?* At this time, a whisp of wind gently blew Jin Xiaomei's fringe. Instinctively, Jing swept her hair behind her ears. Suddenly their eyes met. He clearly saw the love for him in them.

Xiaomei was embarrassed under his direct gaze. She said half angrily, "Close your eyes." "Why?"

"Do not stare at me like that!"

"Alright, I will close my eyes." Wang Jing closed his eyes, obeying Xiaomei's order.

"If I left, would you remain here all night for me to return?" she asked.

"No." He immediately opened his eyes, trying to take Xiaomei's hands, but she cleverly evaded his manoeuvres. Jing pretended to be annoyed. She pouted her lips at him.

"You are joking with me again." He said as a bright smile flashed briefly on Xiaomei's face, as if lit by a stray sunbeam.

"Xiaomei, I have a poem that describes how I feel about you.

> *There was once a beauty in the north,*
> *independent and distinguished.*
> *When she smiled for the first time,*
> *all in the city fell to her feet.*
> *When she smiled for the second time,*
> *all in the country fell to her feet.*

You look so lovely when you smile. I hope you will smile forever."

Xiaomei just sighed and moaned, "You embarrass me."

In the thick silence that followed, they heard a man playing the Er Hu (Chinese violin) nearby. The music was tragic but touching. Her emotions confused her. She was telling herself that this should be easy. *He clearly is attracted to me. And I am attracted to him. Why could I not allow what is natural to happen?* She could not. A notion of who she should be was blocking her. Her father would not want her to love Jing. And then this dynamic between her father and his father, her mother and his father, her friendship with Dan Si and her promise to her, the competition of their two chess clubs, and that damn treasure. What is the use of holding all the treasure in your hands if it does not bring happiness? Why was the world full of liars and greed? Why in the beginning was she not allowed to play chess? A tear rolled silently off her cheek.

Wang Jing noticed her tear. "What's the matter? Did I say something wrong?"

"No." Xiaomei squeezed a faint smile.

With determination he said, "I want to see your father, to ask him for your hand."

Xiaomei gazed into Wang Jing's eyes, trying to determine his sincerity. She saw truth in his eyes.

She simply replied with a pain in her throat, "Jing, thank you. But it is impossible. We can only remain friends."

Wang Jing felt greatly troubled. He must overcome her fear. "Why? Are you engaged?" he asked with concern.

Xiaomei did not answer his question but pointed at the old man who was playing the Er Hu. "Some people's lives are as sad as this music. Everything has been predestined long ago. Love often ends tragically."

"You are so wise for your age. But what has that got to do with us?"

She ignored his question and said, "I want to give that old man some money." He nodded and followed her, where she put a few coins in his hands. Xiaomei whispered to him, "Dear Grandfather, you play such wonderful music. Thank you."

The old man looked at Xiaomei wisely and said something which surprised her, "If you are unwilling to marry in the future, take good care of yourself! Learn to be strong and independent."

She was astonished, not knowing what he meant, but at the same time knowing full well what he meant. Her instinct told her that this old man was a seer of some sort. Before she left, she asked the man, "If our family's fight, what shall we two do?"

"It is their business. Heaven will bless you. It is better to forget old grudges and start a new way."

Xiaomei knew what he meant and thanked him. He was quoting words from the *Book of Changes*.

"What was that all about?" Jing asked with confusion.

"He means that I am as beautiful as a blossoming flower in the summer." Xiaomei said, making a face.

"Why not in the winter?"

Xiaomei felt she now needed to be alone, so she smiled and said, "I must go home. It is getting late. Thank you for the game, and the time together." She said this with her mind elsewhere, trying to decipher the words of the old man, "*If you are not going to marry in the future...,*" "*if you are not going to marry in the future...*"

CHAPTER NINETEEN

A BOAT RIDE

The next morning, Xiaomei saw Zhang Zheng enter the classroom. She was keen to see him and thank him for saving her and bringing the prince to the court room. She also wanted to hear what news he may have.

Zhang Zheng told her happily that Rou Rou had not shown his face in the club since the court case. It was assumed that he was at the *Happiness Chess Club*. Wang Wengfeng had lost face. He blamed Rou Rou, and Rou Rou said Wengfeng had used him.

Xiaomei replied, "Rou Rou may have been the source of all their troubles, but Wang Wengfeng was quick to use him. And he is still the Rou Rou's master."

Zheng also told her that since the coach ride, he and the prince had become friends. "We play chess, and he is happy to hear my impressions of what is happening on the street. It seems that he does not trust the version of things his officials tell him and likes my impartial opinions." He made no mention of the prince's desire on Xiaomei.

❧ ❧ ❧ ❧ ❧

Wang Jing and Xiaomei met at the bank of Qinhuai River. It was a river of history, having witnessed the rise and fall of many dynasties. Xiaomei had organised the meeting as she needed to talk to him.

"Do you want to take a ride in a boat?" Jing could see that Xiaomei was contemplative. He wondered why she wanted to see him but was delighted.

"That would be nice." She smiled gratefully. He rented a boat from a local fisherman, and soon he was rowing them down the river. They were quiet as they looked at the white buildings on each side, the gentle breeze brushing their hair.

No matter how troubled she was, she was 'lifted' by nature. Xiaomei suddenly thought of what her mother told her about her birth. She could not help sighing.

"Why do you sigh?" Wang Jing asked, surprised.

She shook her head to indicate she did not want to share her thoughts. She asked, "I have a question. If I were one of those failed women, would you still play chess with me?"

"Of course I would, as long as you were a good player." He took this as a joke.

"I'm serious. What if I am really a failed woman?" Xiaomei looked into Jing's eyes, searching for an answer.

"Whether you were a failed woman, or a siren, or a genie, I would still play chess with you." Wang Jing was still laughing.

"You're laughing at me. Don't."

This time Wang Jing did take notice and felt a pang in his heart, without knowing the reason. *Why did she ask me this question?*

Slightly irritated by his silence, Xiaomei splashed water on his face.

"What are you doing?" Jing laughed and splashed back. Xiaomei tried to block the splashing as the water was chilly.

She spoke again, "It's just a question, as I have a reason to feel sorry for failed women. But it doesn't matter, let it go."

They remained silent, listening to the oars as they hit the water on each stroke. The boat surged along, until she said, "I needed to meet you today to convince you that we cannot be together. And you know the reasons."

Wang Jing's thoughts drifted over the reasons. Dan Si's image flashed in his mind. He remembered how much their parents wanted their engagement. He was almost certain that Dan Si loved him much more than Xiaomei, and that she would even give her life for him. But whenever he was with Jin Xiaomei, he forgot all his worries, the need for money, and even the burden of running the family business in the future. Jin Xiaomei was a match for him in chess. To him, Jin Xiaomei was a mind reader, who could almost guess his every move. He knew of the feud between their fathers. Then he thought of the responsibilities in his life...

"Let's row back." she requested. From his silence, Xiaomei knew that she had received his answer — that he agreed they could have no relationship together. She was relieved but saddened at the same time. She also saw the irony in his conclusion; he was doing exactly what his father did when his father was told he could not marry her mother Wen Wen. That was why Xiaomei asked the question about fallen woman. As much as she loved Jing, she knew her decision was the correct one.

Without saying a word, he turned the boat back to shore. Just before arriving he said, "I love you Xiaomei... but... we will always be friends."

And there he ended it. As she walked home, through the streets, she did not care who saw her tears. Arriving home, she locked herself in her room and sobbed.

CHAPTER TWENTY
WANG JING, WEAK, LIKE HIS FATHER

When Wang Jing returned home, he looked for his father. He had questions he wanted to ask about Jin Tieling and the troubles between them. Before Jing greeted his father, his father said in an angry tone, "It's good you are back. Someone is stirring up troubles in Jiang Hu. I have heard rumours that there is a treasure code hidden somewhere in the manual *The Secret under the Mahogany tree*. God knows why I have been in the dark for so many years."

"What? Treasure?"

"There has always been a rumour about treasure being hidden in Plum Valley. Apparently, the answer is in *The Secret under the Mahogany tree*. It was Jin Tieling who gave the second volume to me." His father said pitifully and angrily, no longer pursuing the lie that master Chong Xu gave it directly to him. "Time was too short, and I never read the first volume of the manual. Anyway, get our volume and let us see what we have missed."

Wang Jing went to the bookshelf. He searched for the manual, only to find it missing. He immediately started sweating.

"Haven't you found the manual yet?" Wang Wengfeng was irritated by his son's tardiness.

"Father," Jing's face was pale, "The manual is missing."

"What?" Alarmed, he jumped out of his seat and looked for himself. The manual was indeed gone. He could neither sit nor stand, too angry to speak. His lips trembled. He suddenly looked old. Jing hurried to support his father into the nearby chair.

Jing's mind was running fast. *He clearly remembered that he only showed the manual to Xiaomei. But it was impossible for her to steal it, because he checked the book before he went to the river, and she was with him the whole time...*

"What are you thinking?" His father noticed the look of thoughtfulness on his son's face.

"Father, I have become friends with Jin Xiaomei, the daughter of Jin Tieling."

"What?" Wengfeng shouted, "You fool. Did she steal it?"

"No father, the manual was here earlier today. In fact, I have just come from seeing her and it was here before I left. Anyway, we have spoken of *The Secret under the Mahogany tree* manuals, and theirs was also stolen some months ago, long before the court case. She and her father believe it was Rou Rou who stole it."

Sudden it became clear, *Rou Rou had been playing him, pretending to be a loyal student until he discovered the whereabouts of the second volume. First, he betrayed Jin Tieling, and now him. What a fool he had been, completely taken in by that young rogue.* He realised that his need for revenge against Jin Tieling clouded his logic. And he even allowed that traitor to remain with the club after the court case. He mumbled, "I have reaped what I have sown. I never should have allowed Rou Rou to join our club."

"Sorry, Father, what do you say?"

"Nothing. Yes, it must be Rou Rou. Go and ask the servants to see if he is still on the premises and find out when they last saw him."

Jing went to do so. Wengfeng sat with his head hanging.

When Jing returned, his father had lit an incense burner. The smoke curled upwards, and the room was filled with a faint fragrance. It had been many years since he lit incense. He looked at his son, waiting for his reply.

"Rou Rou was seen by several servants sitting outside the room where the manual was. It would seem that he saw me leave the premises. Then, some half an hour later, he was seen to be in such a hurry to leave the club that he nearly pushed over old Mr Song who was in his way. He was carrying something wrapped in a silk cloth. He has not been back."

"Nor will he be." Wengfeng exclaimed with anger.

Jing felt his legs shaking, then asked, "Father, when is my marriage to Dan Si to be? I want to marry as soon as we can."

His father relied, "At least you have not become totally senseless. It will be in November."

"Thank you father." As he said this, he turned his back from his father so he could not see the tears that filled the corners of his eyes. He was about to leave when his father said in a gentle voice, "Wait. Sit down. Remember that in chess we sometimes need to lose something in order to gain something more important. It takes more courage to give up, rather than stick to it. Son, I once loved a woman, but I couldn't marry her. It broke my heart. I believe if I were young again, I would have made the same choice. Dan Si is a good girl. Everyone can see that she is deeply in love with you. You are wise to keep her. You must treat her with love and compassion."

Jing nodded his head. He knew his father was right. But how did his father know?

"Now about this competition. I will not be playing in it. Do not forget to practice. You must win. I am counting on you to keep face for our Wang family name."

"Why are you not playing Father. You must!"

"No, not now. I'm too tired. A year ago, I might have. Let that pig Jin Tieling try his luck." As he said this, he realised his words contained less venom than they once would have.

"Xiaomei said her father was not going to play."

"Oh really… Well, let the next generation continue. Between now and the tournament I will play every day with you to get you ready. We might have lost the manual, but we don't want to lose our good reputation. The future credibility of our club is in your hands."

Jing nodded his head solemnly, unhappy with this responsibility. He was so choked with emotions that he could hardly utter a word. After a few minutes' pause, Jing asked, "Father, may I go now?"

"Yes, you may."

ია ჟ ია ია ჟ ია

Jin Xiaomei spent a sleepless night tossing on her bed. Although her decision was made, it was not an easy one to live with. She wondered how Jing was feeling. She hoped Wang Wengfeng and her father would let go of the resentment that had divided them for all these years. Xiaomei felt a spasm in her stomach, but then she remembered the words of the seer near the river, and she relaxed a bit.

The next morning, feeling washed-out, she arose with the dawn. As was her habit she went out to the courtyard and began cleaning. She fed the fish and then went inside to greet her parents. After they had tea together, she went back outside. The sapphire-blue, cloudless sky looked gorgeous. She started to clean the front of the club, which had not been cleaned for a few days. Her first task was to tend to the flowers. Suddenly, she was interrupted by a messenger who handed her a letter. Assuming it was for Father she started to take it inside, then noticed it was addressed to her. It was sealed with the crest of the *Happiness Chess Club*. Pausing her steps, she broke the seal. It was from Wang Jing, and read:

> *Good morning Jin Xiaomei. I bring bad news. Our version of the manual has been stolen. Since we noticed it was missing, there has been no sign of Rou Rou. It would seem that you were correct, he is indeed the culprit.*
>
> *I thought you should know.*
>
> *Sincerely*
> *Wang Jing*

Xiaomei took a deep breath to steady her emotions. Her deliberations were interrupted by Zhang Zheng, "Good morning Xiaomei. It's a lovely day today." He then considered her demeanour, "Is everything okay?"

"I'm fine. But I have just received the news that the *Happiness Chess Club*'s version of the manual has been stolen, probably by Rou Rou. Don't tell Father as he already has enough troubles at the moment. I will tell him in due course." Xiaomei cast a worried glance at her father's room.

Zhang Zheng nodded his understanding.

"So, what's your news?" she asked "I have not seen as much of you lately. I'm getting hungry, you don't feed me anymore!"

He laughed and said, "I am taking the Imperial examination. I have been studying, as the exam is getting closer."

"Good on you. When you pass you'll get a good job in the court."

"Yes, the Prince has already offered me a post." He paused for a moment before bending over to pick up a wildflower from the ground, still fresh with dew on its petals, and carefully placed it in Xiaomei's hair. Xiaomei smiled back gratefully and continued her work, while he headed into the classroom. She would go into the classroom herself soon, as she needed to prepare for the competition.

CHAPTER TWENTY-ONE

THE CONTEST

With the falling of the first leaves, Xiaomei knew that autumn had arrived. The tournament was only a few weeks away. After the students left for the day, Xiaomei and her father devoted their attention to her practice. They occasionally discussed the possibility of the hidden treasure, but not so that they could plan on how to claim it. They were concerned about how it divided the community.

Prince Zhu visited Jin Xiaomei's residence every now and then. At first, it was ostensibly to make sure the club was functioning properly again. But as he kept coming, it was obvious he had other reasons.

Xiaomei treated him with the greatest respect and kindness, but she never mentioned marriage. The prince had his pride and also never mentioned it.

"Thank you for visiting us." Jin Tieling would say to him emotionally. "Sorry about Xiaomei. She is totally absorbed in her chess practice."

The Prince just nod, as if he understood. He would sit and silently watch Xiaomei and her father practice their strategy. On one occasion he asked, "Whose chess skills are better, yours or your father's?"

Jin Tieling was quick to answer, "My daughter plays better than me, but I still have strategy to teach her, when she listens." He said this with a twinkle in his eye. She pretended to throw a piece at him.

When the prince was not there, and all the students were gone, it was then that they spoke and stratagised about each known player, and their ability and tactics. They made lists, and it always came down to Wang Jing, herself, and that scoundrel Rou Rou as the three likely contenders for the title of best player.

They knew that Rou Rou was a better player than he made out to be. And since he was the only player in the dynasty to have studied both manuals, he must be a strong contender. Xiaomei wanted to win the competition, but if she lost, she hoped Wang Jing would beat Rou Rou.

One evening Tieling said, "It is probable that you will play Rou Rou either in the final or the semi-final. Either way you must beat him. We both know that he will learn the best strategy to beat you. But we will play him like he is a child." He said this with a knowing chuckle.

"How Father? If he knows all the moves and strategies, what can we do?"

Tieling chuckled even louder, "We guess which three plays he is likely to use, and we develop moves to beat them. He will never consider this possible."

"But the moves he will use came directly from Wang Siyi. Perfection cannot be made more perfect."

"Chong Xu, our Master, use to teach us that his master Wang Siyi was just a steppingstone. That each generation must improve on the last. Wang Siyi said to our master 'you must be better than me'. Of course, Chong Xu was a good player, but he was not a brilliant player. He was a better teacher, and that is what he taught. But you have the ability. You can do this. You are smart enough to identify every strategy he could possibly try, then knowing this, you can win. Now all we have to do is to work out new advanced strategies. So, get paper and a brush, and let's plot out each of those moves, and work out new strategies. Rou Rou will never think that there could be moves other than the ones he has studied."

As she went to get the materials he asked for, she shook her head in disbelief.

The day before the contest, Jin Tieling called Xiaomei to his study and gave her a final lesson, "You are you ready. You know that."

Xiaomei nodded her head firmly.

"How are you going to open the game?"

"It depends on who I play. Jing will play losing the initiative. Rou Rou will first play gaining the initiative, then he will quickly stake out his strategy."

Jin Tieling smiled and said, "Some final advice. You need to attack your opponents' weak positions by showing your fist in the game."

"I will keep it in mind." She said politely.

"Good. If you meet a strong player who seems more powerful than you, how are you going to win?"

This time her response was a little less polite, "I will not confront him directly."

"Remember, you are to play chess with men. Many have a bad habit. They won't feel satisfied unless they have hunted down and eaten all the pieces on the chessboard."

"I shall always remember that I only have one goal in my mind: to win the game. I'm not going hunting." Jin Xiaomei said with a touch of impatience.

"Um. Another thing…" he was about to offer more advice, when she cut in, "Father, I am ready. You can't make ready more ready. Together we have devised new strategy. You must relax… calm down." She smiled at him, and he realised he was more nervous than if he were to play himself. Embarrassed, he quickly changed the subject. "Regarding the second poem in *The Secret under the Mahogany tree.*"

"Yes." She recited it from memory. "What of it?"

Tieling said, "I'm quite sure the treasure is hidden in the cave in Plum Valley. According to the highlighted words — battlefield, war, chariots, horses, Han dynasty, and River — if you enter the cave, I think that there may be a chess puzzle to solve to gain access. Only a chess master will be able to pass." Jin Tieling continued solemnly, "I know it is heavy for you, but you must shoulder this burden. Master Chong Xu gave the manual to me, hoping that I would take care of the secret, but alas, I gave the book to a third person, causing all this trouble. Imagine what would happen if the treasure fell in the hands of villains?"

They both fell into silence as they considered the implications. "Daughter, whatever happens, I am proud of you."

Xiaomei nodded her head in the same solemn way. She knew it was up to her to protect the treasure. Her father was too old.

The contest took place in the huge garden pavilion of Prince Zhu Wenchun's residence. The news about the contest aroused incredible interest and was the subject on everybody's lips. Even the emperor had been overcome by a child-like glee. When he heard Prince Zhu's pronouncement of the tournament, he instructed officials to draw up a programme and rules. Each chess club was to have a competition to determine its best player. That player would be their representative in the contest. There were sixty different flags prepared, representing the sixty chess clubs competing.

The Mid-Autumn festival inspired a nation. Zhu Wenchun's garden was crowded with excited spectators and players. As happens in China during festivals, there was food everywhere. Some people had bought their own, while others bought from vendors who were scattered around the garden. A seventeen-person dragon paraded to the applause of the crowd. Firecrackers were let off. Many wore their best clothes in celebration. Fortunately, the weather played its part, and the sun smiled in a deep blue sky.

Jin Xiaomei arrived early. She was wearing a light pink top and a white skirt. She looked so tiny that it seemed a gust of wind would blow her over. She was excited and ready for the challenge – she could do no more than to play her best. The fact that she was the only female player put additional pressure on her. She would show them all that a woman could play chess just as good as any man. There was a lot of interest in her, and she was the focus of many stares. Traditionalists looked down on her with arrogance.

Xiaomei had become used to people's prejudice since she started to learn chess — even her father's. She surveyed the masses who came to this event with different intentions.

The blowing of a horn interrupted her thoughts. Then the prince's commanding voice announced, "Players, spectators! Today, we are to hold the first national chess contest since the start of the Ming dynasty. There are sixty chess clubs represented, so the first round will have thirty games. The winner of each game advances into the next round of fifteen matches, and so on. For the finals, the remaining three contestants will play each other. The winner will be called the Chess Master of the Ming dynasty." There was a great cheer. "In addition, we have chess classes for young children up to the age of twelve. Both boys and girls can participate." This time the cheer was not as enthusiastic.

Lots were draws to select who played who in the first round. With a drumbeat, the games started. Thirty tables of players all made their first move. There was a loud cheer. An administrator sat at each game to ensure the game was played fairly, and that time limits for moves were adhered to. Spectators went from game to game, sighing and cheering, smiling and frowning, as players won or lost.

In the children's corner, a hive of children bubbled with excitement as they all wanted to move at the same time. The prince observed the children smiled. It was his idea to have the children's class, and to include girls. Thereafter, he walked to and fro, scrutinising everything to make sure all ran smoothly. He was in his element.

As expected, Rou Rou, Xiaomei and Jing got through their first round, all enjoying easy wins. Losers good naturedly shook hands, and invariably went and consoled themselves with eating festival food, discussing amongst themselves what could have been… if only I made this move instead of that move.

Many people were intrigued and watched the young girl, Jin Xiaomei, who proved to be a great discussion point. The prince's helpers had to keep moving them away from the table she played at so she could have space to breathe. In the end, they set up a rope around her table that spectators were not allowed to pass. All were amazed at her speed of play. Many sighed with pity — after all, she was just a girl.

In the afternoon, the next round commenced. Jing easily won. Rou Rou laughed at the pathetic player he trounced. Xiaomei played the hope of a club from a faraway province. He was one of the oldest contestants, about her father's age. He ignored the fact that Xiaomei was a girl, and focused on his strategy. There were many moves in the game, but the competitor showed no emotion, completely ignoring the crowd. Not once did he look at Xiaomei, just the board. But with control, she commanded the strategic areas of the board and won conclusively. Immediately his king was checked, and for the first time, the old man smiled and looked at her. He stood and bowed his head to Xiaomei, whilst saying, "Thank you for beating me. It was a good game." He then bowed his head again and disappeared into the crowd. Xiaomei also enjoyed the game. She always knew she would win, but the man provided a good challenge nonetheless. And indeed, he was a gentleman.

The next day, the semi-finals began. A crowd gathered close to the remaining tables, curious to see who would reach the final. All were excited.

Although the spectators already knew, an official of Prince Zhu announced that the three qualifying contestants for the finals were Jin Xiaomei, Wang Jing, and Rou Rou. The onlookers applauded the three players. Curious eyes turned to

Jin Xiaomei, marvelling at her beauty, but still not believing that a young girl was able to play chess so well, especially as she was three years younger than the other two. She humbly gave a light smile. Wang Jing modestly acknowledged the applause, but would have preferred to not be a centre of attention. Rou Rou waved like a conquering hero back from the war, celebrating before the final round. He was smug knowing he was the only person in the dynasty who knew both manuals. Nobody could beat him!

Xiaomei ignored the attention and tried to remain calm. She looked at Rou Rou, and instant disgust rose in her throat, like vomit. She felt it for a second, but knew that she needed to push her feelings back if she was to beat him. Her father's voice echoed in her mind, *There is no place for emotion in chess.*

The first of the finals, as determined by pulling straws, was between Jin Xiaomei and Wang Jing. The winner would play Rou Rou.

They took their seats opposite each other. It was determined that Jing would move first. Wang Jing chose the red pieces. For a second their eyes locked. The tournament was the first time that they had seen each other since the day on the river. In that gaze so much was conveyed. Jing's face was as pale as wax. Xiaomei's was calm. It was almost as if he knew the outcome of the game already. Then at the same time they said, "Good luck. Play your best game."

He moved his central cannon, and Xiaomei responded with a screen horse. He glanced at her and moved an elephant. She was quick to move. Within a few moves she took his horse. He seemed to take longer and longer with each move. With these longer pauses, Xiaomei was able to observe her opponent closely. He seemed to be flustered.

He knew he was not focusing well as he was playing with resentment. He kept hearing his father's voice, *We are relying on you to uphold the family name. You will win!* It had been endless over the previous month. He finally made a move, a silly move. She was quick to pounce and capitalise on his mistake. Within three seconds it was his move again. The pressure was mounting on him. She waited. The seconds ticked by. The crowd murmured. All waited and watched Wang Jing to see what his next move will be. Wang Jing sat there stiffly, thinking. His thoughts were not on his next move. He had lost the game long ago.

Suddenly, he smiled to himself. A decision had been made. To the astonishment of the crowd, he stood up, and said, "I concede."

Xiaomei was shocked.

His father, who stood nearby, had been watching the game attentively. Seeing his son unable to make a move he felt confused. When he heard his son say "I concede", he immediately flew into a rage. He wanted to slap his son, but restrained himself. Instead said, "You coward. You give up when playing a girl?"

Jing, his face stern said, "Father. You would not enter the tournament, but still you blame me. I love chess, but I don't have to win so you can save face. I have played a good tournament and come third in the entire dynasty. Here, you take my place, finish my game. You beat this girl... if you can."

There was a hum from the crowd — everyone knew how Wang Wengfeng pushed his son. Now his son, a man, had pushed back. However, they did think it was strange that he surrendered to a girl. Was he bewitched by her beauty? Or was there a secret behind the relationship between those two families? Among all the guesswork and speculation, Xiaomei put on an expressionless face, looking as if she did not care at all. Jing bent his head down to Xiaomei's ear and whispered, "Destroy Rou Rou." He then left the grounds.

Zhu Wenchun's nerves were stretched tight. He was afraid that this crucial incident would affect Jin Xiaomei. He cast a few nervous glances at her, but she did not show the slightest sign of unease. He felt relieved. He then announced, "The *Happiness Chess Club* concedes defeat. The winner is Jin Xiaomei. She will play Rou Rou for the dynasty title. There will be a break of half an hour before the start of this final game." Prince Zhu Wenchun quickly crossed to Jin Xiaomei and whispered, "Are you alright?"

"Yes." Xiaomei gave him a reassuring smile. Zhu Wenchun was much relieved and hurried off to make some arrangements.

Xiaomei left the table and passed through the still buzzing crowd. She headed for a quiet spot in the garden and sat behind a tree so she could not be seen. Her father knew he would find her in nature, and tracked her down easily, sitting beside her, saying nothing. Content to let her know he was with her and to leave her to her thoughts.

She was proud of Wang Jing for what he did and did not blame him. His father said that he was a coward. On the contrary, he showed great fortitude. She could only accept the situation and play her best game. She would fight in that game to the very end if she had too.

Back at the chess table, Jin Xiaomei narrowed her eyes, measuring the traitor up and down. Other than the competition, she had not seen him since that time in the *Happiness Chess Club* when he waited to steal their volume. He could not look her in the eyes. It was time to reveal the real master.

She knew that he was likely to want to win in glory. If he was to use his central cannon, then it would indicate that he wanted to win in thirteen moves, by sacrificing one horse. She and her father worked out a strategy to not only interrupt his play, but to compromise his position. She would not fall into the trap of taking his horse, but rather disrupt his strategy by moving her chariot to take his cannon. It was Jin Tieling who made this breakthrough strategy, but the method would only work if the combination of Rou Rou's first moves indicated he was moving towards winning in thirteen moves. If he employed another method, then the strategy would not work, and Xiaomei would be forced to rely on her normal skills.

The prince offered the straw selection to see who was to have the first move, but Xiaomei graciously waved the straws away and indicated that Rou Rou could go first, even though he would have the initiative by doing so. She wanted to see his first move.

Rou Rou smiled his devilish smile, and without deliberation used his central cannon to directly attack Xiaomei. Xiaomei knew at that point that he wanted to try and win in thirteen moves. She made a move, and to Rou Rou it looked defensive. Inwardly he smiled, *twelve moves to glory*. Both were fully absorbed in the game. Rou Rou soon realised that the crowd was against him, as when he moved there was not a sound, whereas when Xiaomei moved there was loud hum of approval. It got louder with each of her moves. This made him angry.

On a few occasions, he cast angry looks at the crowd. Xiaomei was not aware of the crowd.

Rou Rou followed the script, move for move, and as he did, his position appeared progressively stronger. Xiaomei stuck to her strategy, and by doing so she seemed to lose ground and several pieces. She was so focused that she was not concerned. The crowd showed signs of worry. Jin Tieling's face was as blank as a closed book, but his hands were shaking. He kept them hidden.

Rou Rou was too eager to win. *Four moves to glory.* He was now enjoying himself, and started to smile at the crowd. Then he moved his second chariots to come in line with the other chariot. Jin Xiaomei lost another piece. The crowd gasped. The prince was like a child whose sweet had been taken away from him. He kept looking at the board, then Xiaomei's face. It was inscrutable. She ignored Rou Rou's trap and knew exactly what to do. She confronted his soldiers with a general.

Rou Rou began to feel confused. *It had been too easy to get to this commanding position. Three moves to go.* Not so confident, his nerves became tight. *What was she up to?* He began to sweat despite the mild weather. The astute audience was aware of this, even though he seemed to be in control. She made her next move and captured a minor piece to occupy it's space. This confused him. Again, he wondered, *what is she doing?* Xiaomei still had the same easy calm focus. He made what he thought would be his second to last move. *One more move to glory.* He hunched over the board, almost unable to control his excitement, willing her to hurry so he could explode in glory.

At first, she smiled to herself, almost imperceptibly, as she leant back in her chair. Then her smile grew. Anyone observing Jin Tieling would have seen the same release of tension. She surveyed the crowd. It was all in slow motion. The crowd, the colour, all waited, confused and silent, all watching Xiaomei. She looked at Rou Rou. He still did not know. He gave a quivering smile, his face twitching. Then, equally in slow motion, the crowd saw her pick up and place her remaining horse. She held it for a moment. Her chariot was in the perfect place after his last move. She placed the horse in the corner square of the board for an 'elbow knight' move and announced, "Checkmate."

For a split second there was silence. Then, seeing that Rou Rou had no answer, the crowd roared in delight. She had won in eleven moves!

Jin Tieling rushed to his daughter, unable to contain his excitement. With tears in his eyes, he hugged her whilst she sat. Then he stepped aside to allow her to be honoured by the cheering people.

Wang Wengfeng had remained to watch the final. He wanted Rou Rou to be soundly beaten. But it went against the grain for him to cheer for Jin Xiaomei. Yet, in the end he was silently mollified. Now, seeing his old friend, his old enemy, standing in front of him, their eyes locked on to each other. Wengfeng gave an almost imperceptible nod of congratulations to Tieling. Tieling returned the nod.

Rou Rou was stunned. He still could not work out the sequence of movements that had led to his demise. So close, but always so far from winning.

"Excellent!" The emperor, who came for this last game, shouted. He knew enough about chess to know that a new strategy had been devised. "This is incredible!"

Zhu Wenchun sighed with relief and announced, "Our esteemed emperor, ladies and gentlemen, players and masters… The Ming dynasty has a new Grand Master, Miss Jin Xiaomei." The crowd roared with delight. "I am sure," he continued when they had quietened down, "that Grand Master Wang Siyi would be delighted to hand over the title to this amazing player." The crowd cheered again.

Jin Xiaomei was calm. The wind softly blowing her fringe. She had a light smile, happy that she had pleased the audience. She went to the emperor and kowtowed for a second, then turned to the prince and did the same. She then headed to her father and kowtowed to him for at least ten seconds. Upon straightening up, she lifted his arm towards the sky, as if to show he was the power behind the win. He surveyed the crowd with a pleased look, his eyes laughing with joy.

Rou Rou did not wait for the ceremony and slunk off like a beaten dog.

Zheng was there. He smiled at Xiaomei when he caught her eye and mouthed, "Congratulations." She smiled back, and mouthed, "We'll chat later when this craziness is over."

The old man who she played in her second round came over and slapped her back in congratulations. His face beaming with happiness. He then chatted to Jin Tieling for a few minutes, as if they were old friends.

CHAPTER TWENTY-TWO
THE FINAL GAME IN PLUM VALLEY

Jin Tieling scanned the crowd, trying to see where Rou Rou was. His sharp eyes spotted him heading out of town, towards Plum Valley.

Rou Rou had waited for the crowd to be occupied in celebration. Together with six or seven henchmen, he headed towards Plum Valley. They were in a hurry. Instantly, he knew the reason — they were going after the treasure. Knowing Rou Rou had the entire manual, and therefore the poem, he knew he would try and retrieve the treasure before the crowd realised he was gone.

He crossed to his daughter and whispered in her ear. At this point, Zhu Wenchun touched her sleeve, trying to have a word with her.

Hearing this, she looked at the prince, "Sorry Prince Wenchun, that crook Rou Rou is going after the treasure. I must hurry."

"You mean you are going to Plum Valley?"

"Yes, I must hurry." As she said this, she put on her walking shoes.

"I'm coming. I don't want you to be alone with that dog."

"What shoes are you wearing? We have a long way to go over some rough terrain."

"These are fine. They won't hold me up." And with that they hurried towards the valley. Xiaomei walked so fast that Prince Zhu could hardly keep up.

Xiaomei followed her father's instructions. A few miles out of the city, there was a brook. Cross the brook and go upwards against the stream and you will enter a beautiful valley, overshadowed by a mountain. Small insects flew along the water surface. A large waterfall descended like a silver thread from high up the mountain.

They were now heading up the valley and could see the group in front of them. Xiaomei was too anxious to notice the beauty of the valley.

She remembered the poem:

*Of chess on the **battlefield**,*
is it a play, or a drama?
If you know how to play with chess pieces,
you command three armies of military might.
*The movement of **chariots** and **horses***
traced back to the Zhou dynasty,
*other pieces have the title of the advisers of **Han** nationality.*
*The **general** plays an important role:*
To remove or appoint the three armies.
*Troops cross the **river**,*
moving quietly with stealth.
A frown emerges on my face as I look back…
I laughed at myself
Every chess game is a trifle of vanity.

"We are gaining on them," Zhu Wenchun was puffing hard but determined to not hold her up. He was not used to walking such distances. Xiaomei just nodded, too intent on searching for the cave with a gate.

"How far do you think it is?" Zhu Wenchun lingered a little behind. Xiaomei said nothing and continued leading the way.

"What are we actually looking for, what kind of place is the treasure hidden in?"

"A cave. We have a poem which gives hints about the cave." Xiaomei recited the poem to Wenchun, who was surprised by the tale.

"Do you mean there's a code in the poem?"

"Yes. The treasure was collected during the war against the Mongols. It was Dan Yu, the son-in-law of Wang Siyi, who fought the Mongols and gained the treasure through his battles. This was what battlefield meant in the poem. 'Chariots and horses' refers to the location of the cave. Father told me that he once found a cave with a gate when he stayed in Plum Valley. Father says that there were two terracotta horses and a chariot at the cave entrance, and that the cave is located near the slowdown of the brook in the valley. Father also guessed there may be traps set up by the Grand Master. We must be careful."

The prince gulped, "OK, we will take it slow. I wonder where Rou Rou and his thieves are? They seem to have disappeared."

The woods covering the mountain hid the cave well, but they finally found it. It was secluded and well-hidden. Being early autumn, the leaves had not started turning yet. The sunshine dappled through the canopies of trees. As they walked towards it, she heard, "Look there." She looked towards where the prince's arm pointed. Just beyond the cave was an abandoned cottage. They stepped inside, only to find the cottage covered in spider webs and dust. "Yuck," Xiaomei complained. They went to the cave mouth. At the gate of the cave, sure enough, there was an abandoned chariot and two clay warriors dressed as Han dynasty warriors. They were life-size and held guard at the gate. This fit the description of the poem:

> *The movement of chariot and horses*
> *traced back to the Zhou dynasty,*
> *other pieces have the title of the advisers of Han nationality.*

"After what you said about dangerous traps, do you think we can go inside?" Zhu Wenchun asked with concern.

"I don't know, but we will know soon."

Suddenly, Rou Rou, Jia Tianjing, and the other thugs jumped out. All held knives towards the couple. "Stay still or die." said Jia Tianjing. "Thank you for showing us the way to the cave. We saw you coming and hid until you passed. Then we followed you." Rou Rou sniggered as he pointed his knife at Xiaomei.

Xiaomei did not answer but looked at them with disgust. Her mind was running fast, trying to figure out how to escape this situation.

Rou Rou felt Jin Xiaomei's gaze on him. It made him uncomfortable. He sniggered again. Jia Tianjing said, "We will collect the treasure – you will get nothing."

"But we showed you the way. We should have equal share." Prince Zhu offered, hoping his title would impress the treasure hunters.

The latter giggled at his naivety. Jia Tianjing laughed, and said, "Who is going to know if we kill a prince and a lady in this wild place? I think this is an ideal burial site, with beautiful nature to keep you company." Jia Tianjing drawled his words, and held his knife steadily, hoping to terrify them.

Prince Zhu, scared witless, fell into a dignified silence. Xiaomei gave Wenchun a meaningful look. Instantly, the prince knew the implication of them going into the cave. The fools knew nothing of the traps. "If you kill us, you will be caught. My father knows we are here. He knows we were following you. It was he who saw you leave the tournament. If anything happens to us, they will look for you. We don't want the treasure. All I ask is that you return the two volumes to us of *The Secret under the Mahogany tree*. We will leave this valley as soon as we recover our lost manuals, if you have them."

Jia Tianjing worried about what she said about Jin Tieling knowing their whereabouts. Hearing Jin Xiaomei's words, he hesitated and looked to Rou Rou for advice. Rou Rou looked at Jin Xiaomei with narrowing eyes, pondering whether or not he should believe her.

Jin Xiaomei added earnestly, "If you don't believe us, you can see for yourselves. We will walk away with the manuals. We don't care about the treasure."

"So, what shall we do?" Jia Tianjing looked at Rou, waiting for his decision. Rou admitted to himself that he did not want to shed blood, so he nodded his head. "Leave them outside! Let's go into the cave and claim our fortune!" Before Rou could stop them, the thugs forced the gate of the cave open, and rushed inside. Rou Rou and Jia Tianjing followed, leaving Xiaomei and Zhu Wenchun outside.

Xiaomei sighed with relief after narrowly escaping death. They settled down and decided to wait and to see what happened. Prince Zhu Wenchun asked, "Are you really happy for them take possession of the treasure?"

Jin Xiaomei joked with irony, "My dear Wenchun, do you not have all the jewels and valuables in your residence that you will ever require? Why die for more?"

Zhu Wenchun blushed as he knew her logic was right. But said, "I feel it unjust that these crooks are rewarded."

"They could be rewarded in ways they did not bargain on."

"Scary thought. I guess we wait."

It was then they heard the first spine-chilling scream from within the cave. They looked at each other. She said, "Wait for a few minutes to see if they come out." They waited, until they heard the second lot of screams. Then she said, "Let's go in cautiously and see if they are still alive. Hopefully they have triggered all the traps." Wenchun nodded, but not with enthusiasm.

They found a torch, which they lit. As they entered the cave, the shadows spooked them. The cave was deep with a narrow channel, which they followed. Upon turning a corner, they saw the bodies of two of the thugs. Arrows were sticking out of them.

Jin Xiaomei put her fingers to her lips to indicate they should be quiet, as there were still more crooks inside. Zhu Wenchun immediately understood what she meant. She used the torch to see if there were any more arrow triggers. Slowly they continued, the torch showing the way in the otherwise pitch darkness. The further they walked the colder they felt in the depth of the cave.

Suddenly, Prince Zhu squealed, as they came across more dead bodies strewn on the ground. "Are all of these people dead?" Prince Zhu asked in anguish.

Xiaomei said nothing, but drew the torch nearer, "Looks like they are." She said with sadness.

"Who said all are dead?" They followed the direction of the voice and with the light of the torch they saw Rou Rou at a chess board on a stone table. He too was hurt, barely alive, with an arrow sticking out of his shoulder. Blood dripped at a brisk pace, but he was ignoring his injury, trying to work out the right move to gain entrance to a second gate. Jia Tianjing was on the other side of the board, looking wild in the light of the torch. Rou Rou said, "So, you have come for the treasure after all. It was a mistake to leave the two of you alive. Now you think you can loot the treasures for yourself." Rou Rou said with effort.

Xiaomei scoffed, "You still worry about us taking the treasure even though you are more dead than alive. No, we came because we heard screams."

Rou Rou broke down, and tearfully begged for mercy "Please save me! I may be a thief, but I don't deserve death. I promise if I survive, and escape from this dark cave, I will turn over a new leaf."

Xiaomei and Prince Zhu looked at each other and instinctively knew the other's intentions. Xiaomei said, "You spared our lives a few minutes ago, we will help you." With these words, the prince grabbed the arrow, and without too much sensitivity, yanked it out, which prompted an agonised scream from Rou Rou. Jin Xiaomei tore some cloth from her sleeves, and bound Rou Rou's wound to stop the bleeding. The prince took off his outer coat and put it on Rou Rou's shoulders to keep him warm. Rou Rou with a deprecating smile nodded, gratefully.

Xiaomei was looking at the iron gate when she heard Rou Rou gasp. Xiaomei quickly followed Rou Rou's gaze and saw Jia Tianjing in the process of moving a horse. "Stop!" she shouted. Too late. Jia Tianjing had made his move. Instantly, a spear dropped from the ceiling, entering his shoulder and piercing his heart. His eyes bulged in surprise as he died.

Rou Rou shuddered, thankful that it was not himself who moved the piece. Prince Zhu was shocked to see such a tragedy, but said nothing, and kept his composure. Xiaomei also shuddered.

"Bad money brings death." Rou Rou murmured to himself as if a philosopher. Suddenly, he burst out laughing, and sprang to his feet, the prince's coat falling to the ground. His shouts echoing in the cave, "Bad money brings death," he cried repeatedly, whilst dementedly waving his arms. Blood dripped from his shoulder. He ran towards the entrance.

Prince Zhu felt his flesh creep. "He seems to have gone insane. Shall we try to help him?"

"No point. He's probably beyond help." Jin Xiaomei was staring at the chess board. The prince instantly knew what she was contemplating. "No! No you don't!"

"I can solve this move." Still staring at the chessboard and pieces. Xiaomei smiled and without explanation and quickly moved cannon f7 to g6. Nothing happened for a moment, and then the iron gate clunked opened.

"How did you know what the correct move was?" She replied that the moves were from the poem in the manual – *to open the way*. They looked at each other and with the light of the torch they cautiously entered through the gate, safely. A mountain of gold awaited them, shining their most glorious light, illuminated by the torch.

Xiaomei gaze at this golden room, thinking no one would ever believe such treasure was hidden in this wild valley. Never in her wildest dream did she think she would understand the Grand Master enough to make the correct move. She saw a picture of her Grand Master Wang Siyi on the wall and kowtowed to the picture.

Zhu Wenchun looked around the gold-studded room and said, "We are rich."

Xiaomei shook her head, "No, do you remember the last lines of Chen Yi's poem?" Jin Xiaomei quoted the poem *"Every chess game is a trifle strive for vanity.* For now, we will leave it here. Only we know where it is. We will go back and tell the emperor to send troops to claim it. We will urge him to use it wisely to help the poor."

Zhu Wenchun was amazed. The more he knew of this girl, the more she surprised him. "Not only are you eligible to be called a Grand Master, but you also have the sage mind of Wang Siyi."

Xiaomei smiled faintly and said, "Let's get out of here."

When they were leaving the cave, they found Rou Rou's dead body at the cave entrance. Xiaomei searched his body and retrieved the two manuals. Together they started to walk back and enjoyed the spectacle of that glorious valley, when suddenly she stopped. "Wenchun, we can't leave this place until we pay our respects to the mahogany tree. Father said it is a bit further up the valley where Master Wang had his compound."

EPILOGUE

The emperor listened to the report from Prince Zhu, and marvelled greatly at such a young woman's wit and courage. By imperial order, Jin Xiaomei was made 'Grand Master'. She was the only one in the dynasty. The decision was appreciated by all the citizens. The emperor also announced that the *Plum Valley Chess Club* would forever more have imperial sovereignty, and that Jin Tieling would remain as the Emperor's Chess representative for the dynasty. The club was reopened with imperial pomp and ceremony. Visitors and students flocked in their hundreds, and Jin Xiaomei's courtyard was more crowded than ever. Her flowers were looking beautiful. Wang Wengfeng and Dan Si were honoured guests, as was the old player from that far province.

Jin Tieling lived many years. He died a content man. Wen Wen had died some five years before him. Her only regret was that she had no grandchildren to play with.

Jin Xiaomei furnished the chess club tastefully in her own style. She added flower arrangements to many corners, and there was a large statue of her father in the courtyard, with the words on a plaque *Integrity, Honesty, Chess* inscribed. She added many chess and military volumes to the bookshelves. Now, with the two manuals back with their rightful custodian, Xiaomei had a special glass cabinet made to house the manuals — never again would they be separated or hidden from students. The newly created strategies by Master Jin were also on display.

The Plum Valley Chess Club became the most prestigious in the land, where high-ranking officials met to play chess and mingle with players. Business and politics were discouraged in the club. The club was for the students, and they received the best treatment, both boys and girls.

The emperor had listened to the request of Jin Xiaomei, and allocated a portion of the gold from Plum Valley to be used to help the poorer citizens.

Dan Si and Wang Jing married. Dan Si was a good wife and mother, as we knew she would be. Her husband, Wang Jing, was loving and attentive to his wife. Within ten months of marriage, Dan Si gave birth to a boy. Wang Jing named him 'Wang Xiaosong', meaning pine tree.

After the memorable chess contest, Wang Wengfeng retreated behind the scenes and left the management of the *Happiness Chess Club* to his son. He spent most of his time sleeping and refused to see anyone.

The old resentments between the *Plum Valley Chess Club* and the *Happiness Chess Club* vanished. The two new masters met each other occasionally as good friends, talking about the beautiful and adventurous past. And no visit was complete without Jin Xiaomei being asked regale them of her adventures in the cave – Dan Si and Wang Jing, rolled with laughter, as if listening to some ancient legend. Wang Jing and Jin Xiaomei never mentioned their four chess duels with each other, nor did they ever pay a match against each other again.

One day, Xiaomei visited the *Happiness Chess Club*. She was always welcome. There were not many physical changes in the club. Just at that moment, Wang Jing and Dan Si's five-year-old boy ran into the room. As Xiaomei played with the boy, she felt her heart miss a beat. She only then understood why Wang Jing named his son Xiaosong, as her name was Xiaomei. In Chinese culture, both the plum flower and pine tree belong to the three evergreen plants and were regarded as auspicious. Wang Jing still remembered her and kept her name in his mind. She felt greatly honoured. The knowledge that he had managed to preserve some indelible space in his heart for her made her feel good.

At that moment, Dan Si and Wang Jing came out. Xiaomei quickly put on bright smile to greet them, cheerfully hiding her true feelings. She came to the point directly, her smile not disappearing from her face, "I have come to talk to your father."

"It's a little hard. He refuses to meet with anybody these days. He is unwell and doesn't have a good appetite. He has lost a lot of weight." Dan Si said with sadness. "He is an old and cynical man." Wang Jing sighed with embarrassment.

Xiaomei, saddened by this news, said, "Oh well. Please do me the favour of giving this handkerchief to him?"

Wang Jing took the handkerchief, confused.

"Please, give it to your father." Xiaomei smiled "And don't ask questions. Your father will understand everything."

Both Wang Jing and Dan Si looked at each other, before nodding their heads.

"I have to go." Jin Xiaomei got up.

"Why not stay longer?"

"Aha, I have to look after some business at the club." she smiled and left.

Wang Jing gently knocked on his father's door and heard an annoyed croaky voice, "What!" His father looked up at his son, paying little attention to him. "Father, just a moment ago Jin Xiaomei was here. She asked me to give you a handkerchief."

"Who is this Jin Xiaomei?" His father asked confused.

"She asked me to give you a handkerchief."

"What handkerchief?" Upon seeing the handkerchief, he instantly recognised it. He grabbed the handkerchief greedily. As he unfolded the piece of cloth, his eyes grew moist. The love birds on the cloth as vivid as ever. Wang Wengfeng shed old, tired tears for the first time in his life. His mind was absorbed in those days, and he wondered if his old friend Tieling knew that he had two purposes in mind when he asked him to return the handkerchief to Wen Wen. Yes, the first and obvious was to tell Wen Wen what a cad he was. The second, was more obscure, it was with the hope that Tieling would take Wen Wen in. He knew of Tieling's love for Wen Wen. Remembering everything, he tightly clutched the material to his chest and felt the catch in the back of his throat.

A few years after the tournament, Prince Zhu Wenchun married, but not Jin Xiaomei. The two remained best of friends. Zhu Wenchun came to visit her chess salon every now and then, and sometimes brought his latest child. However, to the end of his days, he admitted that he only wholeheartedly loved one woman.

Every Spring Festival, Xiaomei would hike to the mahogany tree in Plum Valley to pay her respects. She would burn incense and sit with her back against the trunk of that old tree. She would kowtow to the image of Master Wang and thank the tree for its resilience when looking over generations of her people. On those days she would return home in the evening nourished and gratified with life.

And as for Jin Xiaomei? She got what she wanted. She sacrificed much for the sake of playing chess. She loved her life teaching the young ones the game that shaped her and her destiny.

Was she able to endure the loneliness of her life? Well, there was often a smiling visitor — Zhang Zheng. He now had a responsible position in the government. Xiaomei knew that Zheng understood her better than anyone else. So…

Now, if anyone was to walk the street where the Plum Valley Chess Club was, they will see a shrine. It is the image of a young lady, set in the Ming dynasty. The young lady has a chess piece in her hand, a slight-side smile enlivens the dimples in her cheek, as she is about to place it for a checkmate.

If you enjoyed this book by Feng Ping, you may enjoy her historical novel *Four Legendary Women from Ancient China* (see www.heartspacepublications.com ISBN; 9780648921530).

APPENDIX

As a chess player of many years, I believe that I know a fair bit about the Chinese version. However, before writing the novel, I conducted a great deal of research into Chinese chess, including its origins, tactics, development, and so on.

Many people believe that chess originated India. However, I hold a different opinion. There is a lot of evidence to support my view. Firstly, the origins of Chinese chess has been dated back to the Zhou dynasty, from 1046 BC to 256 BC. It was developed as a chess game to balance the results of divination. The *Book of Changes* was written in that period. The divination was made based on the *Book of Changes* and the game was initially popular among the high-ranking officials and nobles.

Chinese chess continued developing in the Han dynasty (202 BC-220 AD).

The board for Chinese chess is different to that of regular chess, in as much as there is a 'river' in the middle, which is called 'the border between Chu Kingdom, and Han Kingdom', which symbolised the war between the Chu Kingdom and the Han Kingdom. Liu Bang (the king of Han kingdom) instigated the war with Xiang Yu (the king of Chu kingdom). Therefore, the Chinese empire was divided between the two Kingdoms at that time.

Chess was created to minimise a real war between the Chu and the Han. This has little connection with Indian's chess.

According to my research, Chinese chess evolved into its modern form in the Song dynasty (960 AD-1279 AD) when the final strategies and rules were formed. A new piece was invented then – the cannon. It came about because of the invention of gun powder.

Some people may argue that on the Chinese chessboard, the 'elephant' piece shows that Chinese chess was somehow related with Indian's chess, as that animal was not from China, but the animal did roam in India. In my opinion this is a misconception. Further, the elephant in the Chinese language has similar pronunciation to that of prime minister. So, the elephant can also be named a minster in the English translation.

The elephant is a very important piece in the chess game. It is a defensive piece, which guards the palace from being attacked by other offensive pieces. In my opinion, this is the method of how the various Chinese governments ran things in ancient China. The ministers and the prime minister ran in dynasty by proposing important advice to the emperor. This again indicates the development of the game in China.

So, what is the difference between Chinese chess and chess played in the West, and/or India? Chess that is played in the West came from India. It was developed based on the composition of ancient Indian armies. Through war, trade, and religious communication, Indian chess spread to Europe and developed with time, finally evolving into the current game.

There are many similarities of rules and strategies between Chinese chess and Western chess. Both have thirty-two pieces. The movement of some pieces like the rook (castle), knight (horse), bishop (elephant) and pawns (soldiers) are similar. Some strategies like 'checking the king' are similar.

Some of the differences are firstly, regarding the pieces, Western chess doesn't have:

— a cannon (remember Chinese people invented gun powder long before and then the cannon);

— nor does it have mandarins or advisors. These are two guard pieces next to the King, and serve as defensive pieces too;

— another difference can be seen in the chessboards. On the Chinese chessboard there are strategic positions when playing the game. When moving the rook or other pieces, if it occupies one of these strategic positions, that can put the opponent in a compromised position.

The western chessboard it is flat, in as much as one player marches from their closest border to the opposite border of the opponent's side. This can be explained by the difference between Chinese and Western battles, historically. In the West, especially in Europe, the battlefield was orchestrated, where each army needed to stand opposite each other. The soldiers' courage was much valued in the battle, and so they had this form, almost as if it was a game with rules. While in ancient China, the battle took place on a very complex terrain.

At the same time, in Chinese philosophy, to win a war, all elements must line up 'energetically' such as: the right time (of the battle), the advantage of place, and the harmony of participants. All of these are determined or plotted in advance, so the result is likely to be more auspicious.

— Regarding the strategy, Chinese chess players need to think indirectly in order to win the war. *The Art of War* by Sun Zi is fully embodied in the chess game; while in the Western chess, the strategies are relatively direct, and considered by the Chinese players as rather a cruel and brutal battle.

— Chinese chess does not have a 'queen'. Chinese society, especially in those ancient times, was patriarchal. In Western society, the queen can have great power. Throughout the history of Europe, the political marriage of a queen would always bring the union of two kingdoms. For example, the queen of Poland, Jadwiga, married the king of Lithuania, leading to the merging of Poland and Lithuania, and creating a prosperous Jagiellonian dynasty. Take the British queen, Elizabeth I, as an example. The reason why she refused to marry was because she wanted to have "balance of power" among all the candidate countries, which these marriages would not bring.

— The king of Chinese chess cannot move out of the palace, while the king of Western chess can traverse (one square at a time), and, unless directly threatened, can also attack the opponent's pieces. And, when the king hides behind the castle, it is a strong defence strategy in the Western chess. It is a micro picture of palace life in ancient times.

— There is a difference in the pawn in Chinese and Western chess. In both, the pawns stand in front of the army to protect, and they can move very slowly (one square at a time). If a pawn crosses the end of the board after the last row, it can be rewarded by becoming another more powerful piece. However, in Chinese chess this is not the case. This is because class status must remain intact, and there is no promotion due to achievement. From this we can see the severity of the hierarchal system in ancient China.

As mentioned, chess was definitional. It was played in conjunction with the 'the eight trigrams' from the *Book of Changes*, where a game balanced the results of prediction. For divination, special oracle bones were used. By lucky coincidence, these oracle bones developed into some written Chinese text.

According to the *Book of Changes*, the elements of the world were divided into Yin (female) and Yang (male). In other words, from the materialist point of view, into matter and counter-matter. The Yin (female) and Yang (male) develop into four representations of people's lives. The four images give rise to eight hexagrams. The eight hexagrams developed into sixty-four trigrams. There were six lines, either solid or broken in the middle in each hexagram, with each symbol representing one image or condition. For instance, taking the first hexagram as an example, the Qian hexagram, which is also called the 'Heaven Diagram', explains the various states that a gentleman (only men played) must go through if he wanted to succeed. The statements of this diagram read, '*If a gentleman aims to achieve success, he must work diligently, examining himself every moment, catch each opportunity, and avoid arrogance when he has achieved success.*'

The chessboard consisted of sixteen pieces for each opponent, including two chariots, two horses (Knights), two elephants (Ministers), two advisers, five pawns, two cannons, and a king. Players used various tactics, including exchanging pieces, attacking, surrounding, capturing, tempting, countercheck, and others, to gain the initiative, and to occupy critical strategic points. Playing chess was regarded as one of the four intellectual skills of the most refined societies, along with music, calligraphy, and painting.